Spring Texas Bride

The Brides of Bliss Texas – Book 1

KATIE LANE

To my oldest daughter and spring bride,
Aubrey Lane, your vivacious, giggly
personality never fails to brighten my day

CHAPTER ONE

THE FISH WEREN'T BITING.

Waylon Kendall stared at the red and white bobber, willing it to dip under the sparkling sunlit surface of the pond. When it only wobbled slightly in the ripples kicked up by the wind, he started to reel it back in.

It was a beautiful day, especially for the first week of February. The breeze was nippy, but the Texas sun was hot. A perfect day for fishing—whether you caught a fish or not. Or at least that's what he tried to tell himself. But, truth be told, he never had liked fishing. It bored the hell out of him. His daddy and two younger brothers loved to fish. To them, fishing wasn't just a hobby. It was an addiction. They lived for their fishing trips when they could sit in a boat or on a sunny bank, drink beer, and watch a bobber bob. It helped them decompress from their family responsibilities and the stress of their jobs.

That was exactly why Waylon had grabbed his fishing pole and tackle box late that Sunday afternoon. He'd hoped fishing would help him relax

and decompress. Not from family—unlike his
brothers, he didn't have a wife or kids—but from
his job as the sheriff of Bliss, Texas.

There had been six generations of lawmen in
his family. Six. His great-great-great grandfather had been one of the first Texas Rangers. His
great-great-grandfather, a territorial sheriff who
had captured some of the most notorious outlaws
in the west. His great-grandfather and grandfather
had become two of Dallas's most decorated police
officers. And his father had been the sheriff of Bliss,
Texas, for over thirty-five years before he called it
quits and moved to Austin. Law enforcement ran
strong in Waylon's veins. He was born to serve and
protect.

He was not born to fish.

He finished reeling in his line and checked the
hook. The worm was still attached . . . and wiggling. He felt a stab of sympathy for the bait's
plight. Recently he'd felt like a worm on a hook,
speared through the gut and unable to wiggle free.

Of course, he'd asked to be impaled. The job of
sheriff was an elected position, and he'd put his
name on the ballot knowing that he was a shoe-in.
Everyone in the county knew Waylon would
someday replace his father Malcolm Kendall. And
Waylon had looked forward to the time when he
got to wear the shiny sheriff's badge his father had
pinned on every morning.

But that was before he realized the kind of
responsibility that came with the star. As a deputy for his father, he hadn't felt accountable for
the entire county's safety. If fact, he hadn't taken
his deputy job seriously at all. He'd acted like a

good ol' boy who teased and joked with everyone and believed in issuing warnings and giving second chances. If a person didn't heed his warning, he could always count on his father to step in and actually enforce the law.

Waylon didn't realize his mistake until after he'd won the election and people refused to take him seriously. They expected second chances . . . and thirds and fourths. He'd started feeling like his brothers when they corrected his nieces and nephews. "I'm giving you to the count of three to stop that or else" didn't work. And while there wasn't a lot of criminal activity in Bliss, there was a lot of misbehaving. Misbehaving that, if left unchecked, could lead to someone getting hurt. And Waylon wasn't about to let that happen. He cared about his town and the people who lived there.

So he became tough. He stopped being the good ol' boy who joked and teased and became a hard-ass who didn't issue warnings or give second chances. If you broke the law, you got a citation or tossed in jail. No excuses.

Subsequently, his personal life had gone to hell. He was no longer invited to parties and barbecues. No one wanted the "mean boss" spoiling their good times. Not that he would've attended even if he had been invited. As a deputy, he had been able to take off his badge and become a civilian. As the sheriff, he felt like he was never off-duty.

The sound of crinkling paper pulled his attention away from the wiggling worm. A squirrel had slipped down from one of the oak trees to grab the last piece of his granola bar out of the wrapper. The animal didn't seem to be too worried about getting caught. It stared back at Waylon with big brown eyes as it quickly filled its furry cheeks with honey, oats, and flaxseed. But it did freeze when the dog lying next to Waylon stopped snoring and opened one bloodshot eye. The squirrel had nothing to worry about. The dog was no threat. This was proven when the droopy eyelid closed and the snoring continued.

Waylon had gotten the dog for company. He'd thought that a bloodhound would be the perfect canine detective to help him sniff out crime. But it turned out that Sherlock had a nasal condition that affected his sense of smell . . . not to mention he was the laziest creature in the entire state of Texas. He cared nothing about hunting down criminals or chasing a squirrel that was eating his master's breakfast. All he cared about was food and naptime.

"Crazy dog." Waylon muttered as he scratched Sherlock's floppy ears. He recast his line. But after only a few minutes of watching the bobber, he started thinking about everything that he should be doing. Mowing his lawn. Cleaning his house. Grocery shopping. And the mountain of paperwork he had to do since his assistant Gail had taken an extended leave of absence to care for her aging mother.

He could ignore the household chores, but he couldn't ignore his work. Heaving a sigh, he got to his feet. "Come on, Sherlock. Fun's over." The dog pulled together his miles of drooping skin and slowly followed Waylon to the truck. Waylon had just tossed his fishing gear in the bed when his phone rang.

If it had been his personal cellphone, he would've

ignored it. His mama had been calling a lot lately, dropping not-so-subtle hints about the single women in Bliss who would make wonderful wives. Waylon didn't want a wife. His life was stressful enough without adding to it. But he couldn't deny that he needed a woman. Fishing might not help his stress, but a night of great sex certainly would. Unfortunately for him, sex with a woman from the community was out of the question. He didn't want to walk into Lucy's Place Diner and hear his sexual escapades being gossiped about. He'd worked too hard for the town's respect to lose it because he was horny.

He pulled the cellphone he used strictly for emergency calls from his front pocket and checked the caller ID before he answered. "What's up, Tuck?"

Tucker Riddell had only been his deputy for a few months. He was fresh out of the academy and still a little high-strung and superhero drunk. He thought he was Robin, Waylon was Batman, and Bliss was Gotham City. Still, he was a good kid with hardworking values.

"We got us a situation, Sheriff." Tucker's voice was two octaves higher than normal, which was already pretty damn high.

"Take a deep breath and tell me what's going on."

"It's a 10-32." Tucker liked to use code. Usually wrong.

"Someone drowned?"

"I thought 10-32 was drunk and disorderly."

Waylon opened his truck door and waited for Sherlock to jump in. "Someone is drunk and disorderly? Where?"

"The Watering Hole."

Waylon was surprised. People had gotten drunk and disorderly at the town's only bar before, but usually on Twofer Tuesdays when the entire town showed up for buy-one-get-one-free beer and hot wings. Never on a Sunday afternoon when most folks were home taking naps . . . or fishing.

"Who is it?" he asked.

"Mike and Orville."

Mike and Orville? The two were best friends and had been ever since Waylon could remember. They were regulars at the bar, but had never gotten drunk or caused any problems. Something wasn't right.

"You want me to take them to the jail and book 'em?" Tucker asked.

"No, I'll be there in fifteen."

In less than thirteen minutes, he was driving down Main Street in Bliss. A couple years back, the street had looked like a ghost town. Most of the businesses were closed and the buildings vacant. But then fate had smiled on Bliss, although most folks thought fate had gotten a little help from the ghost of Lucy Arrington.

Lucy was the great-granddaughter of the founder of Bliss. She had written a classic series of novels called Tender Heart in the 1960s based on the mail-order brides her great-grandfather had brought to Texas to marry the cowboys who worked his huge ranch. She'd died before she could write the final book in the series. Or at least, that's what everyone thought until the first chapter of the lost book was discovered. The hunt for the book brought new people into town. People who opened up businesses like Lucy's Place Diner and Home Sweet Home, the home décor shop that sold antiques and Tender Heart souvenirs.

Finding Lucy's final book and the new businesses opening motivated the townsfolk to start taking pride in Bliss. Old business owners gave their storefronts facelifts, and the town council added new lampposts and trees all along Main Street. There was even a new Tender Heart museum that was filled with artifacts from Lucy's life and the lives of the original mail-order brides. Which had made more tourists show up. And added more stress for Waylon.

He pulled into the Watering Hole parking lot and parked behind Tucker's patrol car. As he'd expected, there were only a few vehicles in the lot. He recognized Mike's and Orville's trucks and the Cadillac that belonged to the owner, Hank. He did not recognize the white Jeep Wrangler or the trailer attached to its hitch. No one in Bliss owned a cotton-candy-pink vintage trailer with the words *Spring Fling* printed on the back in scrolled letters.

Waylon studied the i's dotted with daisies for just a second before he got out and gave a command for Sherlock to stay. Not that the dog was going anywhere. He was fast asleep in the backseat.

When Waylon got inside the bar, he found Hank sweeping up glass. The owner nodded toward the poolroom. "I had Tucker take them to the back. I didn't want any more of my glasses broken."

Waylon took his aviator sunglasses off and hooked them in his shirt collar before heading to the poolroom. The light was brighter in the room. Mike sat at one table with a swollen eye and Orville sat at another table with a puffy lip. The men were still bickering. Tucker stood between them with his hand on his gun as if waiting for them to make a move so he could quick draw. All Waylon had to do was step into the room to get the men to shut up.

He pushed back his cowboy hat and turned to Tucker. "Tell me what happened."

Tucker visibly relaxed. "From what I can piece together, they were having a beer and talking about the Cowboys' dismal season when a woman walked in and one thing led to another."

Waylon glanced at Mike and Orville, who had to be pushing seventy. "You two got in a fight over a woman?" It was surprising. Women and sports were the two main reasons for bar fights. But usually it was the younger, testosterone-filled men who lost their cool over a female.

"She was a woman worth fighting over." Mike stood. "She was as pretty as a yellow rose of Texas and would've agreed to be my wife if not for that butthead." He pointed a finger at Orville.

"Barbara Leigh would never have married you in a thousand years," Orville said, as he rose to his feet. "She only went out with you once, while she went out with me three times."

Waylon stepped between the men and pointed at Orville. "Sit down or I'm hauling you in. And I still might once I untangle this mess. Who is Barbara Leigh?"

"Barbara Leigh Fulton," Orville clarified as he sat back down. "She was the homecoming queen of the class of 1967 and married that oil driller from Oklahoma."

Waylon tried to fit the pieces together, but he

was struggling. "And she got a divorce and came back to town?"

Orville shook his head. "Last I heard, Barbara Leigh is still happily married with six kids and thirteen grandkids. She sends Ms. Marble one of them photo Christmas cards every year with her entire family on it."

Waylon was now more confused than ever. "So why were you fighting over her if she's married and doesn't even live here?"

Orville thought for a moment before he scratched his balding head. "Hell, I don't rightly know. We were just sitting there talking with that sweet little gal from Houston about the loves of our lives, and the next thing you know, me and Mikey was going at it."

Suddenly, things became crystal clear. Some troublemaker tourist had come into the bar and instigated a fight between the two friends. A fight that seemed to be winding down.

Mike chuckled. "We sure did get a little hot-headed over a woman who dumped us both." He touched his swollen eye. "That's quite a punch you got for an old man, Orville."

Orville grinned. "You're not so feeble yourself. What say I buy you a drink?"

Waylon could've hauled them in for being disorderly, but they hadn't done any harm besides breaking a couple of glasses. Still, he thought it was best if they stopped while they were ahead. "What say we skip the drinks and head on home," he said. "And on your way out, you need to make restitution with Hank for the glasses you broke."

Both men nodded. "Yes, sir, Sheriff." They walked

out together, slapping each other on the back.

When they were gone, Waylon turned to Tucker. "Make sure Mike and Orville settle up with Hank and leave separately, then you can get back on patrol."

"Will do, Sheriff." Tucker saluted with a click of his boot heels.

Waylon rolled his eyes as he headed out the emergency exit door that led to the parking lot. The Jeep with the pink trailer was still there. He had little doubt that Spring Fling was the one who had started the fight. He couldn't give a citation to someone for instigating, but he could make it clear that he didn't like people causing trouble in his town. He slipped on his sunglasses as he strode over to the little door and knocked. The low-throated bark had his eyes narrowing. They narrowed even more when the door opened and he got a good look at Miss Spring Fling.

Her.

He should've known it would be her. If not by the name, then by the vibrant pink trailer. From the first moment he'd met her, he pegged her as the type of woman who liked to draw attention to herself. The neon blue streak in her short black hair was a dead giveaway. As was her clothing. Today she wore a shirt and a pair of tight jeans that looked like they'd been run through a paper shredder. The tangerine material of the shirt was slitted to reveal the lime green tank top beneath, and the ripped jeans revealed long, tanned legs. Her feet were bare. Her toenails painted a blue as neon as the stripe in her hair.

But it wasn't her neon toes or her ripped jeans

or her striped hair that annoyed him the most. It was the twinkle in her big blue eyes whenever she looked at him. A twinkle that was impish, disrespectful, and impertinent.

"Why, Sheriff Kendall," she said in a voice as bright as her trailer. "What a surprise."

CHAPTER TWO

MEN DIDN'T USUALLY INTIMIDATE SPRING Hadley. But she had to admit that there was something a little intimidating about Sheriff Waylon Kendall. It was probably due to his size. She wasn't short, and if you added the height of her trailer, she should be looking down at him. She wasn't. His tan cowboy hat was eye level, and his broad shoulders filled her entire door. He wore a scowl on his face. A scowl that deepened as he studied her from head to toe and back again. The few times she'd run into him when she'd been visiting Bliss, she'd gotten the distinct impression that he didn't like her. Now she was pretty positive that he didn't.

It was puzzling.

People usually loved her.

The cute hound dog she'd rescued started snoring loudly, and the sheriff's eyebrows lowered behind the top frame of his aviator sunglasses. "Do you have my dog?" The word *dog* came out slow, country, and kind of sexy.

She glanced over her shoulder at the dog lying

on her bed, then back at the sheriff. "That's your dog?" She was surprised. He seemed too uptight to own a laid-back hound dog. Even now, his shoulders were all bunched with tension, and the skin around his square jaw looked tight, like he was clenching his teeth. Her sisters Autumn and Summer thought the sheriff of Bliss was hot. And there was something ruggedly attractive about him. But Spring didn't like uptight guys. She had to deal with an uptight sister and that was more than enough. She liked guys who enjoyed life as much as she did. Guys who knew how to smile . . . and didn't hate her.

"You want to tell me why you stole my dog?" he asked.

"Oh, I didn't steal him. I saved him. The temperature inside a car can get twice as hot as the temperature outside. Which is why when I saw your dog looking out the window with his tongue hanging out, I brought him back here for a nice cool bowl of water." She didn't mention that the dog had completely ignored the water, and instead helped himself to her ham sandwich when she wasn't looking.

The scowl lessened, but the sheriff still didn't look happy. "Both windows were down and it's only sixty-two degrees outside. He wasn't going to get overheated."

She shrugged. "Better safe than sorry." She plastered on her biggest smile and held out a hand. "I'm Spring Leigh Hadley, by the way. Dirk's sister. We met at Dirk and Gracie's wedding."

His expression didn't change. "I remember. You own a clothing store in Houston with your two sisters."

Just the mention of Seasons made Spring's smile fizzle and brought back the fight she'd had with her sister before she'd left town. One little mistake and Summer had exploded like a Fourth of July firework display. Of course, Summer was always exploding about something. She had a short fuse and the temperament of a rattlesnake. Spring knew that, but had still been hurt when Summer had called her an irresponsible ditz who couldn't remember to tie her own shoes. Spring wasn't irresponsible. She'd worked just as hard as her two sisters trying to make Seasons a success. Did she occasionally get distracted and forget things? Yes. But that didn't mean she was a ditz. And Summer would regret her words when she discovered that Spring had left town.

"I do own a retail clothing store in Houston with my sisters," she said. "But I decided to take a little time off and do some camping."

"In a bar parking lot?"

She laughed. "I planned to stop by and see my brother's family before I went camping. Unfortunately, as soon as I hit town, my engine started smoking. And since the only gas station is closed, I pulled in here and called Dirk."

She couldn't see his eyes behind the dark lenses of his sunglasses, but she could feel his gaze boring into her. "And while you waited for your brother, you decided to go into the bar and start a fight?"

Spring was known for her sweet disposition, but the man's grumpy attitude and his rude insinuation pushed her right over the edge of sweet into pissed. Mainly because he was starting to sound just like

Summer—blaming her for something she hadn't done. At least not intentionally.

She crossed her arms. "I don't know what you're talking about. I didn't start a fight. I only went into the bar to get some sugar for my iced tea, and the only people I talked to were the bartender and two nice older gentlemen who told me about the love of their lives. Now if you'll excuse me, I'm going to go back to my lunch." She started to close the door, but he placed a hand on it and stopped her.

"Are you forgetting about stealing my dog?"

Her even temper snapped. "I did not steal your dog!" She whirled in a huff and took the three steps necessary to reach the bed. The dog was sound asleep amid the clothes she'd been in too much of a hurry to pack, snoring contently. She placed a hand on his soft, velvety head and gave him a gentle shake. "Come on, sweetheart, time to go back to your annoying master." The animal kept snoring.

"You'll have to do more than that to wake up Sherlock."

She whirled to find the sheriff standing in her trailer. She'd thought that he looked big outside. Inside, he seemed to take up the entire space, with his wide shoulders squished between the kitchen cabinets and the door to the bathroom and his head bent to keep from bumping it on the ceiling. He had taken off his cowboy hat and sunglasses, and for the first time she got to see his eyes without the shadow of a hat or the cover of dark lenses.

For a moment, she was dumbstruck by the dew-drenched meadows of those beautiful green eyes. Okay, so the sheriff *was* hot. He cleared his throat, and she realized she'd been gawking like a crushing teenager. She pulled her gaze away and looked at the dog.

"Sherlock?"

"A miscalculation." He stepped closer. "If you'll excuse me, I'll get him."

She turned sideways and tried to let him pass, but the trailer was much too small. Or Sheriff Kendall was much too big. There was no way for him to get around her without them touching. For one tummy-tingling second, she was trapped against a hard chest that had no give whatsoever. And when she tried to move past that wall of granite, she couldn't. She glanced down to see the button of his shirt caught in one of the slits of her shirt.

"I think we're hooked," she said a little breathlessly.

It took him a moment to answer. When he did, his voice sound as breathless as hers. "Can you get us unhooked?"

She reached between them, extremely conscious of the hard muscles her fingers brushed against. But she was too close to see what direction to untangle her shirt. "Can you move so we have more room?" she asked.

He put an arm around her waist and lifted her completely off her feet and two-stepped around. The manhandling was disconcerting. Once on her feet, she tried to put some space between them. But it seemed that she'd gotten the button even more entangled.

He tossed his hat onto the table. "Here, let me try." But when his knuckles brushed against the top swell of one breast, he pulled back as if burned and bumped his head on the ceiling.

She couldn't help it. She giggled.

"You think this is funny, do you?" His features were stern, but there was a sparkle of humor in his eyes.

"Hilarious. It's like being in a china cabinet with a bear. Or maybe Alice in Wonderland after she takes a bite of the cake."

One eyebrow quirked. "Eat me."

The witty reply took her completely by surprise, and she couldn't help but giggle again. "So the stodgy sheriff does have a sense of humor."

"Stodgy?"

"How would you describe yourself?" She placed a hand on his shoulder. It was as hard as the rest of him. "Wait, let me guess. You see yourself as the tough, steely-eyed lawman. A true bad ass."

"I am a bad ass."

She cocked her head and looked up at him through her lashes. "You don't look so bad now, Alice."

He hesitated for just a second before he tipped his head back and laughed. A deep, husky laugh that rumbled through Spring like a late July thunderstorm. An electric tingle of sexual awareness zinged through her. In her early twenties, she would've given into that zing and kissed him. But over the years, she'd learned that sexual desire was fleeting. Once the fireworks were over, you were stuck with the person. A person you were either compatible with or you weren't. And from what she'd seen so far, she was *not* compatible with the sheriff.

Unfortunately, everything she felt was usually

written all over her face. Including sexual desire.
This was confirmed when the sheriff finally
stopped laughing and looked at her. Humor died
from his eyes to be replaced with a sizzling molten
green desire that just about melted her panties.

His hands settled on her waist as his head tipped
and lips lowered. For a second, she thought about
letting him kiss her. Just one little kiss wouldn't
hurt anything. But then she remembered Summer's hurtful words about her being a ditz who
acted before she thought, and a breath before their
lips met, she turned her head. She tried to come up
with something clever to say to relieve the awk-
wardness, but she couldn't come up with a thing.
Thankfully, a knock on the door saved her.

Waylon pulled back and bumped his head again
as his gaze snapped to the door. His eyes no longer
looked molten. They looked panicked. He held a
finger to his lips, signaling her to keep quiet. But
Spring had always had trouble taking orders . . . and
keeping quiet. Besides, it was probably her brother.

"Come on in," she called. "The door's open."

Waylon sent her a hard, annoyed look before he
reached between them and ripped his shirt free.
By the time the little old woman in the big straw
hat stepped up into the trailer, he had moved back
against the table and was holding his hat over his
chest.

"So it is you," Ms. Marble said when she saw
Spring. "I figured as much by the name on the
back. Last time I talked with her, your grandmother didn't mention a word about you buying a
cute little trailer."

Ms. Marble and Spring's grandmother, Granny

Bon, didn't live in the same town, but they spoke on the phone at least once a week. Ms. Marble had been Lucy Arrington's best friend. On her deathbed, Lucy had asked Ms. Marble to find her daughter and give her the final Tender Heart book. When Ms. Marble couldn't track down the daughter, who turned out to be Granny Bon, she'd started hiding the chapters for Lucy's nephews and nieces to find. Spring didn't blame Ms. Marble for not looking harder. She believed that all things happened for a reason. If Ms. Marble had found Granny sooner, Spring and her sisters might not have been born. Or Dirk.

She walked over and hugged Ms. Marble, avoiding the wide-brimmed hat. "I haven't told Granny about my trailer yet." She knew her grandmother would want to know where she'd gotten it, and Spring didn't like lying to Granny. She didn't mind fibbing a little to Ms. Marble. "I'm afraid she'll think it's frivolous."

"There's nothing wrong with being frivolous. I think it's adorable. And I love the name." She pulled back, and her alert blue eyes moved over to the sheriff. "I hope I didn't interrupt any Spring Flinging."

Since the sheriff seemed tongue-tied, Spring replied. "Not at all. The sheriff is just here to get his dog."

"Sherlock?" All Ms. Marble had to do was say the name, and the dog's head popped up and his tail started thumping the mattress. He jumped off the bed, pushing the sheriff and Spring out of his way to get to Ms. Marble. The older woman smiled and pulled out a bone-shaped biscuit from the tote bag hanging on her shoulder. At one time she'd taught first grade in Bliss. After she retired she became the town baker and made all the desserts for the diner and the townsfolk's special occasions. Spring just hadn't known she baked for the animals of Bliss too.

"Now be a gentleman," Ms. Marble said as she held up the biscuit. The dog immediately sat and waited patiently for the treat to come to him. Once he was chomping away, she looked at Spring. "So you've taken up dog sitting?"

The sheriff finally spoke. "She was just watching him for a few minutes while I handled a situation in the bar." He jockeyed around Spring. "If you ladies will excuse me." He ushered the dog to the door. "Come on, Sherlock. It's time to go home."

Spring should've let him go, but there was something about the sheriff that brought out the little devil in her. "Thanks for stopping by, Alice." He froze for a brief second before he pulled on his hat and followed the dog out the door. When he was gone, Ms. Marble spoke.

"Alice?"

She waved a hand. "Just a silly joke."

"So is this silly joke why Waylon James was laughing? I heard him clear across the parking lot, and I have to tell you that it did my heart good. I haven't heard him laugh that hard since he took over the job of sheriff."

"I don't think it's the job as much as his nature."

Ms. Marble shook her head. "Until he became sheriff, he was always laughing and teasing with the townsfolk. He loved attending functions and being part of the community. Now he rarely smiles

CHAPTER THREE

"THEY'VE GROWN SO MUCH SINCE I saw them at Christmas." Spring cuddled Lucinda close and kissed her niece's chubby little cheek before placing her back down on the colorful play rug and picking up Luana to cuddle and kiss. Then she did the same for Luella. She didn't want any of her nieces to feel left out.

As a triplet, Spring had felt left out plenty of times. She didn't blame her mother or grandmother. When there were three identical babies vying for attention, it was easy to overlook someone. Which probably explained why Spring was such an extrovert. She learned early on that being bright, vivacious, and chatty got her attention.

"They're growing too fast." Her sister-in-law Gracie sat on the floor with Spring and her daughters. For having had triplets close to nine months ago, she looked amazing. She'd lost all her baby weight and appeared fit and happy—if not a little tired. Of course, three babies would tire out anyone. "Luella already has six teeth, Lucinda has started talking, and Luana is pulling herself up," she said. "She was standing in her crib last night when I went into her room to check on her."

"It's nice that they each have their own room."

"Dirk insisted on it. He said you and your two sisters always had to share a room, and he didn't want that for his girls. But sometimes the only way to get them to stop crying is to let them sleep in the same crib together."

Spring understood completely. Since leaving Houston, she felt like pieces of her body were missing. She and her sisters had not only shared a room growing up, but they'd shared a dorm in college, and then later apartments in Houston. This was the first time they'd been apart for any length of time, and Spring felt like a boat without its oars.

"It's better if your girls have their own space to start with," she said. "It will make it much easier if they ever have to separate."

Gracie must've read the sadness in her voice because she reached out to squeeze her hand. "Autumn called and told us what happened. It was a simple mistake, Spring."

"No, it wasn't." She handed a teething ring in the shape of a giraffe to Luella, who was drooling all over the front of her sunflower onesie. "It was much more than a simple mistake. How can a business owner forget to lock up her business? Summer had been right to get mad. With the increase of online shopping, Seasons is already struggling to make a profit. If someone had robbed us blind, we would've had to close for sure."

"But you weren't robbed blind. Autumn said that not a thing was missing when Summer got there the following morning and found the back door unlocked."

It was too bad that Autumn hadn't been the one to open the store that morning. She was the calm and collected sister. The one who never raised her voice or lost her cool. She probably wouldn't have even mentioned anything about it to Summer. Then Summer wouldn't have called Spring a ditz and Spring wouldn't have gotten hurt and ended up leaving. But as Granny Bon always said, "*What ifs* are a waste of time and energy. It's the present moment that counts." And at the present moment, Spring was here in Bliss . . . missing her sisters.

"I apologized," she said. "All I want is for Summer to apologize for the things she said to me. But she refused. And I'm starting to wonder if she does think I'm a ditzy idiot."

"Of course she doesn't. She loves you just as much as we all do. Summer's just a little . . ."

"Hot tempered and stubborn as the day is long," Spring finished the sentence for her. "Which is why I decided to take a little camping trip. Once I'm gone, she'll realize how important I am to the business."

"So that's why you want to go gallivanting across the countryside in a ham can? You want to prove your worth to Summer?" Dirk entered the room. He had changed from the clothes he'd picked her up in—probably because he'd gotten them greasy while checking out her engine. He now wore a white t-shirt, faded jeans, and socks. There was a no-shoes rule in the nursery.

When they saw their daddy, all three babies immediately released squeaks of delight and started crawling toward him like tiny turtles racing for the sea. With an expertise that said he'd done it numerous times before, he scooped up two in one arm and one in the other. "Hello, beautiful ladies. Did you miss your dear old daddy?"

"It's only been a couple hours, Dirk," Gracie said, but her eyes twinkled with love.

"A couple hours are a lifetime to a baby." He gave each one a kiss. "My girls need to know that their daddy loves them every second of every day."

Spring's heart melted, and she couldn't keep tears from welling in her eyes. She knew why her brother wanted to make sure his children knew that he loved them. He didn't want them feeling like he and his sisters had—uncertain of their father's love.

Holt Hadley hadn't been the best father. In fact, he hadn't been a father at all. He'd left right after she and her sisters had been born and only showed back up when he needed money . . . or sex. Which was how her mother had gotten pregnant with Dirk. Her siblings couldn't forgive him. But Spring had never been one to hold a grudge. Like her mother, she believed in giving people a second chance.

Holt had done some bad things in his life, including trying to steal Gracie's brother's ranch. But Spring truly believed he felt bad about trying to take the ranch and being a bad father and was trying to turn over a new leaf. He hadn't called to ask her for money once in the last year and had a respectable job selling RVs and trailers.

Which was exactly how she'd ended up with her trailer. She'd driven to San Antonio to make sure he hadn't lied about having a job, and he'd talked her into the vintage trailer. She hadn't needed a trailer. She had never gone camping in her life. But when his eyes had turned sad and he'd started talking about how much he wished he'd gotten to take his kids camping when they were little, she'd pulled out her checkbook. He'd given her his employee discount and thrown in the custom paint job for free. But even then, it had come close to cleaning out her bank account. Until her fight with Summer, she'd planned on trying to sell it on Craigslist. Now she felt like she deserved a Spring Fling.

"It's not a ham can. It's a vintage trailer." She got to her feet and kissed Dirk's cheek. "Thanks for picking me up, baby brother, and trying to fix my Jeep."

"I'm not sure it's fixable. The transmission and radiator are shot, the battery is corroded, and the tires are bald. How much did you pay for that piece of junk, anyway?"

She wasn't about to tell him. He was the money manager in the family. He also knew how to make it. His online job search company, that he'd started with his friend Ryker Evans, had made him millions. But no matter how much money he had, he still believed that a penny saved was a penny earned. While Spring believed that a penny spent was much more fun.

"Not much," she said. "The guy at the used car lot gave me his best price." She took Lucinda from Dirk.

He snorted. "I just bet he did. Damn, Spring, I wish you'd called me first."

"Don't cuss in front of the girls." Gracie stood

and took Luana from him. "And your sister doesn't need to call you every time she buys something. She's a big girl. She can make her own decisions, including going camping by herself." She looked at Spring. "But I hope you're going to stay for a while. I can certainly use a little help with the girls."

Dirk looked hurt. "Don't I help?"

Gracie patted his cheek. "Of course you do. You're a wonderful daddy. It's just that you've been kind of busy with the ranch and your city council meetings." She looked at Spring with pride in her eyes. "Joanna Daily is trying to talk your brother into becoming Bliss's next mayor."

Spring wasn't surprised. Dirk had always been a leader. The type of man who liked to take charge. For some reason, an image of Sheriff Kendall popped into her head. Now there was a man who liked to take charge. And she couldn't help wondering what would've happened if she'd let him take charge of a kiss. She mentally shook the thought away and returned to the conversation.

"I think you'd make an amazing mayor," she said.

"I'd have to be better than the current one." He blew bubbles on Luella's neck until she giggled.

"Don't be too hard on Randall Gates," Gracie removed a strand of her long blond hair from Luana's fist. "The only reason he took the job was because no one else wanted it."

"I don't get why Joanna Daily doesn't do it," Dirk said. "She does everything else."

"I think if she took on another job, Emmett would divorce her. She's busy enough coordinating the volunteer helpers at the museum and planning the spring dance. I tried to help her at the museum this morning, but the girls decided they weren't going to take their morning nap. And I don't think people like to hear wailing babies when they're trying to enjoy Bliss history."

"You should've called me," Dirk said.

"It wasn't a big deal." She handed him back Luana. "But you can watch them now while I go start dinner."

"I'll help," Spring said.

"No, you stay and visit with your brother."

When Gracie was gone, Spring turned to Dirk. "It sounds like you could use a nanny."

He set the girls on the floor and sat down behind them. "I agree. But it's not easy finding someone in a town this small, and Gracie isn't willing to trust the girls with someone she doesn't know well. For that matter, neither am I." He pulled out some plastic building blocks from an antique chest that had once belonged to Lucy Arrington and started building towers for the triplets to knock down.

Spring placed Lucinda in a circle with her sisters, then sat down. "I'll be more than willing to nanny until I leave to go camping."

"Why camping? You've never shown an interest in it before. You won't like it. You've never liked being alone."

She didn't. Which is why she planned to call her daddy and see if he'd meet up with her. After getting the trailer, she'd started daydreaming about camping with her dad—cooking wienies over an open fire, telling ghost stories, and making s'mores. And when she got back, maybe she could prove to her siblings that Holt had changed. That he was making an effort to be a father.

"Have you talked with Daddy?" she asked.

Dirk shook his head. "After he tried to take Cole's ranch, I want nothing to do with him ever again." He glanced at her. "I hope you haven't been talking to him either. I know you have a forgiving heart, but he's trouble, Spring. I lived with him. I should know."

Spring didn't know all the details of what had happened when their father had custody of Dirk. But she knew that living with Holt couldn't have been fun. While she believed that he had turned over a new leaf, at that time he'd had a lot of problems, including being irresponsible and horrible with money—traits she was afraid she shared.

"Sometimes people can't help getting into trouble. Sometimes trouble just follows you. It seems to follow me."

"Trouble doesn't follow Holt. He makes it." Dirk stopped stacking blocks and looked at her. "And don't you even think that you're anything like our father. Holt is a dark cloud that snuffs out light, while you are a ray of sunshine that always makes people smile. Yes, you can be easily distracted at times, but you would never hurt anyone intentionally."

She blinked back the tears that welled in her eyes. "I didn't mean to leave the door unlocked. I was just late for my hot yoga class, and then Autumn called to remind me to pick up some things at the grocery store, and then I saw that sad man who lives in the alley. He looked so cold that I ran back inside to get him a sweater. It was a returned sweater with a hole in the sleeve so I don't know why Summer got so upset about it."

He put a comforting arm around her and tugged her close, kissing her head like she was one of his daughters. "You always have been so soft hearted. You might get distracted, but it's usually because you're more concerned with other people's needs than your own. Summer and Autumn know that about you. Which means that what happened was as much their fault as yours."

She pulled back to stare at him. "Are you saying they shouldn't have trusted me to close the store?"

"It's not about trust. It's about giving the right jobs to the right people. No matter how much education, training, and experience a person has, some people do not make good managers. And guess what? That's okay. Most of us are better foot soldiers than generals."

Spring sent him an annoyed look. "I guess I'm a foot soldier and Summer's the general."

"Summer shouldn't manage the store either." He picked up Luana, who had started to fuss when she no longer had a fistful of her sister's arm and bounced her on his lap. "Autumn should be the manager of the store. She's focused, organized, can make decisions, and is empathetic without being a pushover. Unfortunately, there's that entire birth order thing. And having been born first, Summer is convinced she should be in charge." He paused. "Which is why Seasons is never going to succeed."

Spring's eyes widened. "What? But you loaned us start-up money. Why would you do that if you thought it would never succeed?"

Dirk shrugged. "Because you're my sisters and I want to make you happy. Besides, would you have listened to me if I told you it wasn't going to work?"

She thought for a moment. "Autumn might've."

He laughed. "But she wouldn't have been able to persuade you and Summer. So I thought it was best to let you learn the truth on your own. Sometimes you learn more from failure than you do from success."

She wanted to argue about Seasons failing, but deep down she knew that he was right. Autumn had been saying the same thing for months. Spring and Summer were just too stubborn to listen. Spring should've felt heartsick that the business she'd been working so hard at would eventually go under. But surprisingly, she didn't feel that upset. She was more upset for her sister.

"Summer won't accept defeat until the bill collectors evict us," she said.

Dirk nodded. "I know. The woman is almost as stubborn as you are." He glanced at her. "You seem to be set on this camping trip. I wouldn't mind if you were going with an experienced camper, but you don't know the first thing about camping. And I don't like the thought of you being all alone in the wilderness."

"Maybe I'll pick up a handsome hitchhiker," she teased.

"You do, and I'll take you over my knee."

She laughed. "Stop being a worrywart. I'll be fine. I'm not actually camping out under the stars. I have my little trailer. How much do you think it will cost to fix my Jeep?" When Dirk quoted a price, her heart sank. He must've read her worried expression because he heaved a sigh.

"You don't have enough to cover it, do you?

What happened to your share of the advance from the final Tender Heart novel?" Each member of Lucy's family had been given a share of the book advance. It had seemed like a lot until Spring had starting spending it.

"I bought my trailer. And then I had to buy the Jeep to pull it with, because my Kia wouldn't have pulled it around the block." She paused. "And then there were a few credit card bills that I needed to pay off."

Dirk arched a brow. "I thought we talked about you getting rid of those and only spending cash for things you needed."

"Nobody uses cash anymore, Dirk. That's archaic."

"That's smart. Especially for a woman who has trouble with her spending."

Since she couldn't argue the point, she conceded. "You're right. I need to curtail my spending. But for now, could I get a small loan? I can't call Summer and Autumn and ask for money. I don't want Summer adding to her list of grievances against me." She sent him a hopeful look. "Just until I get my next paycheck? Please."

"Peas." Lucinda mimicked.

Spring laughed. "See, even your daughter wants you to loan me money."

Dirk sent her a skeptical look. "Or maybe she's just hungry."

CHAPTER FOUR

WHAT DO YOU HATE MOST about the dating process?

Waylon stared at the question on the screen of his laptop. At the moment, what he hated most was answering the stupid questions on the online dating application. He skipped the question and moved on to others that were just as stupid. *What's your favorite movie? Who are your favorite authors? What are some of your pet peeves? What really makes you laugh?*

Spring.

It was surprising how quickly the answer popped into his head. Probably because Spring *had* made him laugh. At least he'd been laughing until she'd looked up at him with big blue eyes that held so much heat he'd felt like a deep-fried chicken wing. Then all the humor of the situation had drained right out of him, and he'd wanted to dive headfirst into that heat and never come up for air. If Spring hadn't turned away, he would've done just that.

Which was why he'd decided to join the millions of other people who Internet dated. It was obvious by his reaction to Spring that he needed a woman in a bad way. And it was better to take his time and be selective about the type of woman he got in a relationship with than to jump in bed with a woman like Spring.

Spring Hadley was trouble. Trouble with a capital T. He knew it the first time he'd laid eyes on her. She'd been a bridesmaid in Dirk and Gracie's wedding, along with her two sisters. But she'd been the only triplet who had short hair with a stripe in it. The only one who'd forgotten her bouquet and hiked up her dress, flashing more than a little leg to the entire church, and sprinted back to the bridal room to get it. And the only one who'd winked at him as she'd walked down the aisle.

Waylon wasn't one to judge a book by its cover, but when Spring had proceeded to flirt with every man at the reception, he'd figured her cover was fitting. He'd known girls like her. Even dated a few. They were never satisfied with one man's attention. They wanted the entire male population to fall at their feet. Which was usually where the trouble came in. And after he'd only just won the townsfolk's respect, he wasn't about to mess it up by getting involved with trouble.

He returned his focus to the questionnaire and typed out quick responses. *My favorite movie is Robocop. Favorite authors are Grisham and Crichton. Pet peeves are people who are late or unorganized.* Since he couldn't come up with an answer for what made him laugh, he skipped that question and moved to what he hated about the dating process. *First dates.* He more than hated them. He despised them. There was nothing more awkward then trying to have a conversation with a woman you didn't know. Or with one you did know.

Having grown up with three brothers, women were like aliens from another planet to him. He didn't understand their preoccupations with their weight or social networking or reality television. He didn't understand their mood swings or their need to talk about every emotion that passed through their bodies. Just because you felt something didn't mean you had to talk about it.

Of course, he wouldn't ever understand them if he didn't make the effort.

He moved onto the next question. *What's your main goal in joining an online dating site?* At the moment, it was to get laid. But since he couldn't put that, he typed something that sounded a little less caveman-ish. *To find a woman who shares my same interests.* Hopefully, that included sex.

"You look pretty intense, Way. Are you hunting down the town's most wanted or Internet shopping?"

Waylon glanced up from computer to see Raff Arrington standing in the doorway smiling. It was good to see his friend so happy. Raff had been through some tough times in his life and deserved happiness.

Waylon closed his laptop before waving his friend in. "Just looking at new fishing poles before I call it a day."

Raff sent him a skeptical look as he sat down in the chair in front of Waylon's desk. "Since when do you like fishing? You never could sit still long enough to let a fish bite."

"I've gotten a little more patient in my old age

and thought I'd give it another shot. What has you stopping by so close to suppertime?"

"I was on my way to pick up Savannah from Home Sweet Home when I saw your light and thought I'd stop by and ask you a favor."

"Shoot."

Raff relaxed back in the chair and swiped at the dirt on the knees of his jeans. Ranching was hard, dirty work, but Raff seemed to love it. And he was good at it. His Tender Heart Ranch was thriving. "It seems Luke has gotten it into his head that he wants to play high school baseball."

Luke was a seventeen-year-old who lived with Raff and Savannah. A year earlier, Waylon had picked up Luke for breaking into Raff's barn. It turned out that the teenager had been running away from his abusive stepfather. Raff had taken the kid in, and once he and Savannah got married, they became like parents to the teenager. In fact, the entire town had taken an interest in Luke's well-being. Waylon included.

"And what's wrong with baseball?" he asked.

"I don't have a problem with him playing baseball. I just don't want him getting his feelings hurt when the coach benches him."

"Why would the coach bench him?"

Raff ran a hand through his hair. "I've been to some of the practices and Luke is pretty bad. I'm talking Matthew Jorgenson bad."

Matthew Jorgenson had been a geeky kid whose dad had forced him to try out for baseball. The poor kid's tryout had been so pathetic it had prompted a catch phrase. Anytime anyone screwed up royally on the field, it was called "Pulling a Jorgenson."

Waylon blew out his breath. "Well, shit. Why did the coach let him on the team in the first place?"

Raff cringed. "I asked him to. Luke's confidence is still pretty low and I was hoping it would help his self-esteem. But now I'm thinking it will get even worse if he has to warm the bench the entire season." He leaned up, resting his arms on his knees. "The only solution is to get Luke better. And since you were so good at baseball, I thought you could give Luke a few pointers."

Waylon *had* been good at baseball. So good that he'd been drafted right out of high school. But his father had talked him into going to college first, and his junior year he'd torn his Achilles tendon and lost out on the draft. Occasionally, he thought about what might have been if he'd gone to baseball straight out of high school. The traveling he would've done. The places he would've seen. But it never did anyone any good to look back.

"I haven't played since college, Raff. I don't know how much help I'd be."

"You're better than I am."

He grinned. "I'm glad you've finally accepted the fact that I'm a better athlete than you are."

Raff took the bait. "In baseball. I kicked your ass at football. The proof is up on the wall in the high school gym."

"You got the record for sacks only because I was out that season with a dislocated shoulder."

"Wienie." Raff's eyes twinkled.

Waylon bit back a grin. "Showboat." He sat up and cupped his hands on the desk. "Fine, I'll try and help Luke."

Raff grinned. "Thanks. But we can't let Luke

know that you're coaching him. He doesn't think he's bad, and I don't want his feelings hurt. Nor do I want him getting pissed. He has a worse temper than I used to."

At one time, Raff had been the most hot-tempered kid in town. Anything could set him off. Thankfully, he'd mellowed with age. Or with marriage.

"Savannah has certainly tamed the bad boy," Waylon said. Raff didn't even try to deny it. "So how are we going to hide the fact that I'm coaching Luke?"

"I thought you could come out to the Tender Heart Ranch under the pretense of helping me with the new addition to the cabin."

"You're adding onto the cabin?"

"I decided to enlarge the kitchen and main living spaces." Raff paused. "And add a nursery." When Waylon's eyebrows lifted, he nodded. "Savannah's pregnant."

The words were lacking the kind of excitement they should hold, but Waylon understood why. A few months back, Raff had confided in Waylon about all the miscarriages his mother had suffered and how each loss had affected his family. It had explained a lot about Raff's volatile mood swings as a kid. And his delinquent behavior. He had gotten into a lot of trouble growing up. He'd also been a good friend who was always there when Waylon needed him.

Waylon got up from his chair and walked around his desk to place a hand on Raff's shoulder. "It's going to be okay. Savannah is not your mom."

"I know that." Raff released a long sigh and ran a

hand through his hair. "It's just hard to forget. Hard to act like I'm not worried sick."

Waylon wished he had some advice to give, but he knew nothing about women and babies. "When do you want me to come out to the ranch?"

"Whenever you can. I do want you to look at the plans for the cabin and tell me what you think. It would be easier to build a completely different house, but Savannah loves the cabin." He smiled. "For looking so high maintenance, she's a simple girl."

Waylon narrowed his eyes. "And I'm still pissed about you stealing her away from me." It was ongoing joke between them. Waylon had only gone out with Savannah once. And she'd made it perfectly clear that she wasn't interested in him.

"Yeah, well, to the victor go the spoils." Raff got up and slapped Waylon on the shoulder before he headed out the door. "See you on Saturday—and bring some balls and a mitt."

When he was gone, Waylon finished up the questionnaire before he tackled emails and the pile of paperwork. He missed his assistant something fierce. Gail was not only organized and efficient, she took care of him without putting her nose in his personal business. The temp agency he'd contacted had yet to send someone to take her place. And even if they did, he was sure they wouldn't be as proficient as Gail.

It was close to eight o'clock by the time he glanced at the time. He was starving and thought about stopping by the diner to eat, but then decided he needed to get home to Sherlock. Joanna Daily and Ms. Marble were his neighbors and took turns keeping an eye on the dog for him during the day. Still, Waylon felt guilty if he got home too late. Sherlock was afraid of the dark.

He shut down his computer, then got up and grabbed his hat from the hook. Before he locked up, he read the sheriff's code of ethics that hung on the wall. It was something he did every night before he left. Something his father had taught him.

"As a law enforcement officer of the great state of Texas, my fundamental duty is to serve the community, to safeguard lives and property, to protect the innocent against deception, and the weak against oppression and intimidation. To keep the peace and—"

His work cellphone rang. It was his other deputy. "Hey, Jonas."

While Tucker was young and gung-ho, Jonas was old and jaded. He'd planned to retire with Waylon's father, but his wife had passed away a few months before and Jonas had needed the routine of his job to get through his grief. Waylon understood this, but it was still hard to deal with a crotchety, depressed old guy who liked to call him out on all the things he didn't do right.

"Your father always answered the phone with his name," Jonas said. "It gave the caller a sense of his authority."

Waylon rolled his eyes. "I knew it was you, Jonas. I have caller ID."

"Still, it sounds official and appropriate for a sheriff."

He took a deep breath and slowly released it. "Sheriff Kendall here. What's going on?"

"Someone broke into the Tender Heart museum.

I was doing my usual patrol when I noticed some-one slipping in the back door."

"It's probably one of the Arrington women or Joanna Daily."

"That's what I thought, but I don't think those women would leave the lights off and break things. And I definitely heard glass breaking."

"Did you go inside and see what was going on?"

Jonas released an exasperated sigh. "That's not how your father taught me to deal with a suspected burglary. I was to call him first and get backup."

Waylon gritted his teeth. "Fine. I'm on my way."

When he pulled into the back alleyway behind the museum, he found Jonas waiting in his patrol car. Or not waiting as much as napping. His deputy was sound asleep and snoring as loudly as Sher-lock. The man really needed to retire so he could take catnaps whenever he wanted. Of course, he seemed to be getting away with that on the job.

Instead of waking him, Waylon left him sleep-ing and headed to the back door of the museum. Once inside, he realized Jonas was right. The lights were off, and it sounded like someone was moving around in the dark.

He reached for the light switch by the door. It was already flipped up, which meant that the power was out . . . or had been purposely shut off. He unsnapped the safety on his holster and moved closer to the wall of the storage room. He peeked around the doorway that led into the main museum. A pinpoint flash of light caught his attention. It bounced along the floor and over the antiques.

With adrenaline pumping through his veins,

Waylon drew his gun and slipped into the room. As his eyes adjusted to the darkness, he was able to make out a form moving through the rows of antiques. He maneuvered until he was behind the intruder. He was about to say *halt* when the intruder ran into something.

"Shit!"

Waylon immediately recognized the voice. The tension left his shoulders, and he holstered his gun. "I should've known it was you."

There was a clatter of something hitting the floor, and the light went out as Spring released a scream. Not a little shriek, but a bloodcurdling scream that made the hairs on Waylon's neck stand on end. He had to yell to be heard over the din.

"Calm down! It's me. Sheriff Kendall."

The screaming cut off and was followed by a release of breath. "You scared the crap out of me. What are you doing sneaking up on a person like that?"

"What are you doing sneaking around the museum in the dark?"

Before she could answer, Jonas came huffing in. "Sheriff Kendall!"

"I'm okay, Jonas."

"What was that scream?"

"I accidentally surprised an Arrington."

Jonas snorted. "So it was one of them girls. What was she doing sneaking around in the dark?"

"It seems that the power is out. Why don't you call Mick at the electric company and let him know? Then you can go home and get some sleep. I got this handled."

"Fool woman," Jonas muttered on his way out.

CHAPTER FIVE

"I WASN'T THE ONE WHO DROPPED it." Sheriff Kendall didn't seem the least bit remorseful about breaking her cellphone.

"No, you were just the one who scared the living daylights out of me." She squinted at the light. "And could you get that out of my eyes?"

The flashlight lowered. She blinked until the dots of light disappeared and she could see the outline of the sheriff's cowboy hat and broad shoulders. "What are you doing here?" he asked.

Since she was getting pretty sick and tired of being interrogated by the sheriff, she was a little confrontational. "I don't think I need a reason to be at my great-grandmother's museum."

"The museum might be named for your great-grandmother's series, but you don't own the building or any of the antiques. Most of the antiques belong to Raff Arrington. And the building belongs to Zane."

"And both men happen to be my cousins and could care less if I'm here."

"Then you won't mind if I call them and ask."

Before he could reach for his phone and bother her cousins, she told him the truth. "If you must know, I stopped by to get Gracie's diaper bag. She left it here this morning when we were helping sell tickets, and she needed Lucinda's pacifier or my niece won't sleep tonight." She held up the key ring and jangled it. "So I have permission to be here, Sheriff Kendall."

"Do you also have permission to break things?"

She cringed. Obviously, the sheriff had stepped on the broken glass on his way in. "It was an accident. One I'll be happy to pay for." She sincerely hoped that the lamp she knocked off the dresser hadn't been expensive or she'd have to ask for a bigger loan from her brother. "Now if you'll excuse me, my niece is waiting for her passie." She tapped the flashlight app on her cellphone, but nothing happened. It looked like she'd have to add the cost of a new phone to the loan.

The sheriff took her elbow. "Come on. I'll help you look."

As much as she wanted to decline, she didn't have much choice. She followed beside the sheriff as he flashed his light over the antiques. They finally found the diaper bag in the back room on a shelf right by the door. It was just another thing that pointed to Spring's incompetence. If she'd been more observant, she wouldn't have had to go into the museum and she wouldn't have broken a lamp and her phone . . . or had another run in with the sheriff.

Sheriff Kendall pulled the huge bag off the shelf. "Damn, this is heavy. What does Gracie have in here?"

"All the things you need to keep three babies happy." She went to take the bag, but he held onto it.

"I'll carry it out for you. Where's your car?"

"At Emmett's garage being fixed. I drove Gracie's. I parked on the street thinking that the key was to the front door, but it turned out to be to the back."

He shut off the flashlight and slipped it in the holder on his belt before he held open the door for her. "So how's the museum doing? It looks like more and more tourists are showing up every day to go through it."

"Gracie said it's going great, and Joanna Daily's idea of using volunteers to sell tickets means that the town gets a bigger share of the profits."

He waited for her to lock the door. "Mrs. Daily is one smart, competent woman. I tried to hire her to help me out at the office for the next couple weeks while my assistant is on leave, but she's too busy with everything else she does." He nodded at the sheriff's SUV parked in the alleyway. "I'll drive you around to your car." Before she could decline, he herded her over to the passenger side like a sheep and opened her door.

Once inside, she took note of the immaculate interior. There were no empty Starbucks' cups or fast food trash like there were in her Jeep. The dash didn't have a speck of dust or the carpeted floors one stain. It looked like the sheriff ran a tight ship. She watched as he walked over and double-checked the door she'd locked.

Tonight, he was wearing his sheriff's uniform— tan felt cowboy hat, tan button-down shirt, creased jeans, and polished black boots that matched his belt and holster. As he turned and strode back to the SUV, once again, she felt a ping of sexual awareness. It confused her. She wasn't a girl who went for men in uniforms. She preferred bad boys in rock and roll t-shirts and tattered jeans. Guys who were interested in a good time and a few laughs. She didn't go for serious stuffed shirts.

While she was trying to figure out her body's reaction to Sheriff Kendall, he got in the car and glanced at her.

"What has you so puzzled?" He handed her the diaper bag. "Don't tell me you left something else inside."

"No. I was just thinking." She glanced around for anything to get her mind off sex and the sheriff. She noticed the gadgets on the dash. "Can I turn on the siren?"

He cocked an eyebrow at her as he started the engine. "This vehicle is not a toy. And the siren is only used in emergencies."

"Oh, come on. Don't tell me you haven't used the siren before when there wasn't an emergency." She shot him a wide-eyed look. "Not even to impress a pretty girl?"

"Not even then." He put the SUV in reverse. "My daddy would've tanned my hide. That, and you're the first woman who's ever asked."

"I bet there were women who wanted to. They were just too chicken to ask."

He glanced at his rearview screen on the dash and backed up. "And I guess you're not scared of anything."

"No, that's Summer. I'm scared of a lot of things."

He expertly wheeled the car out into the side street, then put it in drive and headed for Main Street. "Like what? What's your biggest fear?"

She thought for a moment before she answered. "Disappointing my family." She hadn't intended to be so brutally honest, and he seemed as surprised by her answer as she was. He stopped at the corner and turned to her. She expected more questions. The man loved to interrogate her. But instead, he just nodded.

"Funny. That's mine too." Before she could get over her surprise, he pointed to a switch on the dash. "Flip it, and then push the button next to it. And if you tell anyone, I'll say the crazy Hadley triplet did it without my permission."

"Liar, liar, pants on fire," she teased before she did as he'd instructed. The lights flashed as the siren whined. She got to enjoy the thrill for only a few second before Sheriff Kendall removed her finger from the button and turned off the lights. She laughed. "Party pooper. I bet it's a kick in the pants to do it while going ninety miles an hour down the highway."

He flashed her an impish grin that said he wasn't as straight-laced as she thought. "Which is one of the reasons I wanted to be a lawman." He drove around the block and parked behind Gracie's car. When he turned to her, all the impish boyishness was gone, and the stern sheriff was back. "Now do you think you could stay out of trouble until you leave?"

She shrugged as she opened the door. "I'll try. But I can't make any promises."

Spring got Lucinda's favorite pacifier home in the knick of time. Gracie and Dirk were just putting the babies to bed. She helped by taking Luella to her room and rocking her. Once her niece was asleep, she didn't place her back in her crib. Instead, she cuddled Luella close and thought about what a shame it was that her mother would never get to rock her granddaughters.

Dotty Hadley had loved rocking her children. Granny Bon had a big old rocker recliner that was perfect for a slim woman and her four small kids. As they rocked, Dotty would sing all the popular songs from the radio, some country and some pop, until Spring and her siblings fell asleep. Spring didn't know how her mother got them all to bed. Granny Bon probably came in and helped. All Spring remembered was the contented feeling of being squeezed tight in her mother's arms with her siblings.

On the night her mother died, Spring had rocked in that old rocker and cried her heart out. Around midnight, Summer had joined her. She hadn't cried. Summer wasn't one for tears. She'd just held Spring and taken over the rocking. Autumn had joined them an hour later, and then Dirk. The following morning, Granny Bon had found them all sleeping in the chair like a litter of motherless kittens.

The thought of her grandmother had Spring getting up and tucking Luella in for the night. Once in the guest room, she called Granny Bon. Just hearing her grandmother's voice brought tears to her eyes.

"It's about time you called me back, Spring Leigh Hadley."

Spring started to use the excuse of her phone being broken, but then stopped. Granny didn't care for excuses. Besides, Spring *had* been ignoring her grandmother's calls. Like Dirk, Granny Bon was not going to be happy that Spring had left her sisters to run the business while she went camping. Granny Bon didn't believe in vacations. She believed in family and hard work. She should be retired, but she still worked every day at a transitional home for orphaned children. Having been an orphan herself, she knew how important it was to make the children in her care feel loved. She was a little tougher on her grandkids. And Spring figured she was going to get a stern lecture, so she jumped in first.

"Before you get after me, I want you to know that Summer said some horribly hurtful things. She can't treat people like that and get away with it. I've worked just as hard as she has to make that business successful. And yes, I made a mistake. But it's not like she's never made mistakes in her life. And I know you've been calling me to try and get me to go back to Houston, but I just can't do it, Granny. I'm not going back until Summer apologizes."

There was a pause before Granny Bon spoke. "I couldn't agree more."

Spring glanced at her phone to make sure she was still talking to her grandmother before pressing it back to her ear. "Excuse me?"

"I agree. Summer shouldn't talk to you the way

she does. That girl is way too controlling for her own good. And I have to take responsibility for some of it. After your mama died, I had my hands full. I was grieving and I had to work and take care of four children. Summer has always been responsible and mature. So I relied on her to help me keep an eye on the rest of you kids and keep you out of trouble. I didn't realize she'd take the job to heart. Or that you would allow her to continue bossing you around long after you became full-grown women. I've been waiting for the day you'd get the gumption to stand up to Summer and say 'enough is enough.'"

Spring was almost too shocked to speak. "So you're not mad at me for leaving Houston? You don't mind if I take a couple weeks off to go camping?"

"I think camping is pure foolishness. You need to get a job and start making your own way."

"A job? I have a job. I'm just taking some time off from it."

"You don't have a job. You and your sisters are playing store with Dirk's money, and it's time you stopped playing and grew up." Spring cringed. She'd forgotten how direct her grandmother could be. And Granny Bon wasn't finished yet. "I hated Holt getting custody of Dirk and taking him away from us, but now I have to wonder if it wasn't the best thing that could've happened to that boy. He's the only one of you kids who has his own life."

"I have my own life, Granny Bon!"

"You do not, Spring Leigh. You have Summer's life. She was the one who got it into her head to open a retail store in Houston. She just bullied you and Autumn into tagging along with her. And none of you are happy because of it."

Spring was too stunned to speak. Probably because her grandmother's words hit so close to home. It *had* been Summer's idea to open the store. She was the one who'd decided on Houston. The one who'd had Autumn looking for a vacant building. The one who'd made Spring ask Dirk for the loan. Spring and Autumn had just been foot soldiers carrying out General Summer's battle plans. And still she couldn't stop herself from arguing with Granny Bon, probably because if she didn't have the life Summer had chosen for her, she didn't have a life at all.

"I might not have wanted to run a store at first, but I don't mind doing it now."

"You don't mind? That doesn't sound like a person who loves her job."

"Okay, maybe I don't love it. But Autumn and Summer need me. If I'm not there, the store will fail for sure."

Granny heaved a long sigh. "Maybe it's time you failed together so you can succeed on your own. I realize you're the baby girl of the family. The smiling sweetheart who everyone likes to coddle. But coddling doesn't build character. It makes you weak. It's time to get strong, Spring Leigh. It's time to stand on your own two feet. Now I need to go. I've got another call." She hung up, leaving Spring feeling like she'd been smacked in the face with a tether ball.

She fell back on the bed and stared up at the ceiling. Did everyone in her family view her as a ditzy weakling? It certainly seemed that way. And what was her grandmother thinking when she said Spring should leave her sisters? She could never be happy without her sisters. They had a special bond. All she wanted was a little time away from Summer's nagging and an apology.

She got up and went in search of Dirk. He was in his study working on his laptop. She walked into the room and sat in the chair across from his desk. "I just talked with Granny Bon."

He nodded. "I know. I just called her and she said she'd been talking with you."

"She's crazy, right? I mean, I don't want to leave my sisters forever."

Dirk leaned back in his chair. "I don't think that's what she's saying, Spring. I think she just wants you to have some time away from Summer and Autumn so you can figure out who you are."

"And that's what I intend to do." She sent him a hopeful look. "Just as soon as you loan me the money to get my Jeep fixed."

Dirk studied her with sad eyes. "I'm not going to loan you money, Spring."

"What? But you said that you would."

"That was before I spoke with Granny Bon. Before she made me realize that I'm doing you more harm than good by always bailing you out of things. I loaned you money for the store and look how that turned out. You and Summer are ticked off at each other, and I feel responsible." He shook his head "I'm not going to be responsible if something happens to you on some camping trip. If you want to go, you'll need to pay for it."

Spring's temper snapped. "You and Granny planned this, didn't you? Neither one of you wants me going camping alone so you figured out a way to keep me from it. Well, Granny is right. I do need to stand on my own two feet. That includes not listening to my sisters, you, or Granny. I'm going camping. And if I have to get a job to pay for that camping trip, then I will!"

CHAPTER SIX

WAYLON STARED AT THE EMPTY inbox of his online dating profile. He hadn't thought women would be beating down his door to date him, but he had thought he'd get a few messages, or "hugs" as they called them, from interested women. Maybe he should've given the questions a little more thought. Maybe his answers had been too short and vague. Of course, he hadn't tried to "hug" any women either. He'd found a few he was interested in meeting, but he didn't have a clue how to start a conversation.

This online dating thing sucked.

He sat back in his chair and stared longingly at the empty coffee mug sitting on his desk. Gail always made sure to keep it filled. She also brought him one of Ms. Marble's cinnamon swirl muffins from the diner every morning. Damn, he missed Gail. And damn the temp agency for not sending someone over to take her place. Although he figured it couldn't be easy finding someone who wanted to drive all the way to Bliss. And no one in town seemed to have time to help him out.

He got up and headed to the reception area where they kept the coffeemaker. He grabbed the carafe and filled it up in the bathroom before pouring it into the reservoir and then putting in a filter. He opened the can of coffee, but there wasn't even one scoop left in the bottom. He blew out his breath and threw the empty can at the trash can a little harder than he intended. It rebounded off the wall and landed with a clatter on the floor just as the door opened.

Spring Hadley sailed in, looking like a daffodil in her bright yellow dress and white sweater. "Good morning," she said, as if it were the best morning ever. Her gaze tracked the empty coffee can as it rolled across the floor. "Do sheriffs always start the day off with a little coffee can basketball?"

His face heated at being caught throwing a temper tantrum—especially when Spring looked so smug about catching him. Her blue Arrington eyes sparkled, and her cherry red lips held a definite smirk.

"There's no coffee," he said. The explanation sounded stupid as hell and made her lips twitch with suppressed laughter.

"Then I arrived at the perfect time." She offered him the to-go cup she held in her hand. Steam wafted from the slit in the lid . . . along with the enticing scent of coffee. "Well, go ahead and take it. You look like you need it much more than I do."

He wanted to resist, but his need for caffeine was too strong. "Thanks." He took the cup. The rim of the plastic lid had the perfect imprint of cherry-red lips. He stared at the mark for only a second before he ignored the lipstick and took a deep sip. As soon as the sickeningly sweetened flavored coffee filled his mouth, he wanted to spit it back out. He hated sweet. He was a straight black kind of guy. He had to close his eyes and concentrate to get it down his throat. He opened them to find Spring smiling with satisfaction.

"Good, isn't it?"

He swallowed again to get the taste out of his mouth. "Yeah, real good." He tried to hand the cup back, but she refused to take it.

"No, you can have the rest."

He didn't want to insult her after she'd been so charitable, so he nodded and set the cup on Gail's desk. He'd dispose of it later. "What can I do for you?"

Her smile got bigger. "The question is, what can I do for you?"

The blatant sexual innuendo almost had his mouth dropping open. He'd seen the desire on her face the other day in the trailer, but when she'd turned from his kiss, he figured he'd read her wrong. Now he realized that the desire had been there, and he had to admit that it boosted his ego. Especially after the dismal response he'd gotten on the dating site. Of course, he couldn't take her up on the offer. He had a reputation to uphold. And Spring Hadley wasn't respectable as much as she was unpredictable. She proved this when she reached out and tapped him on the nose.

"Get your mind out of the gutter, Sheriff. I'm not talking about sex. I'm talking about working for you. I'm here for the job."

He didn't know what surprised him more, the fact that she'd read his mind or the fact that she wanted to work for him. "Excuse me?" he said.

She straightened her shoulders and smoothed the skirt of her dress. "I'm here for the job." When he just stared at her, she continued. "The assistant job? The one you told me about the other night? You said that your assistant was on leave and you'd asked Mrs. Daily to help you, but she couldn't because—"

He cut her off. "No."

Her eyes widened. "No, you didn't tell me that?"

"No. I don't want you being my assistant."

Her smile wavered. "But why not? I thought you needed help."

"I do, but the employment agency is sending someone over. Now if you'll excuse me, I've got paperwork to do." He headed for his office, but he should've known he couldn't get rid of her that easily. She followed right behind him, the heels of her canary-yellow shoes clicking on the tile floor. Who wore yellow shoes? He took a seat behind his desk, calmly cupped his hands on the stack of paperwork he needed to get through and repeated himself.

"No."

Her expression went from bright sunshine to scowling storm cloud. "You're just being difficult. The employment agency is not going to send anyone. If they were, that person would be here by now. And from what I've heard in town, no one wants to work for a grumpy sheriff who doesn't smile. Even Joanna Daily would rather spend time with your dog than you."

His jaw dropped. That's why Joanna hadn't taken the job? She didn't want to work for him? And the rest of the town felt the same?

Spring's eyes softened. "I'm sorry, but I think you need to know that no one is jumping out of their panties for this job. And you forgot your coffee." She set the cup of disgusting coffee on his desk, bumping his laptop in the process. The online dating screen popped up. He made a grab for it, but she pulled the laptop out of his reach. The sunshine smile came back. "You're online dating?"

"No." It wasn't a lie. He hadn't gone on one date. He stood and reached over his desk to take the laptop from her. Unfortunately, Spring had already gotten an eye full.

"No wonder you don't have any responses. That has to be the worst picture ever. Did you take it yourself? If you did, you need a lesson in selfies. You never take a selfie straight on. It makes your nose look huge and gives you a double chin. You need to hold your phone above your head and take the shot from a higher angle." She opened the small purse hooked over her shoulder and took out her phone. "Here, let me take another one." She frowned at the cracked screen. "Dang. I forgot. You broke my phone."

He closed the laptop with a snap and sat down. "I did not break your phone. Now you need to leave. I have work to do."

She put her phone back in her purse and picked his up from the desk. She had absolutely no boundaries. She held it up. "Say Cheetos."

"You're not taking my—"

"Too late." She lowered the phone and tapped the screen. "Eeesh. You look even madder than you did in the one you used. And you have something on your top lip."

She squinted at the phone before she laughed. "Women love lipstick, but usually not on men." She waltzed around his desk and took his chin in her hand. Her thumb swiped over his top lip in a heated brush that left him speechless . . . and semierect. Or maybe it was her close proximity that had his body heating. She stood between his spread knees, the full skirt of her dress spilling over his thighs. His hands actually started to tremble from the desire to span her trim waist, and he had to tighten them into fists to keep from doing so. It was a relief when she stepped back and held up the phone.

"Smile, sheriff." She clicked off another couple pictures, and then scrolled through them. "Wow. You are not photogenic at all, are you?"

He held out a hand, thankful that it was no longer shaking. "Give me my phone."

She shrugged and handed it to him. "Fine, but I'm just telling you. You won't get any responses with a picture that makes you look like a Cyrano de Bergerac serial killer. Now about that job. If you hire me, I'll not only bring you delicious coffee every morning, but I'll redo your dating profile until you have women beating down the door for a chance to date Sheriff Waylon Kendall."

"Thanks, but I can get my own coffee and my own women."

One jet-black eyebrow arched. "Then why are you on a dating site?"

He opened his mouth to reply before he realized he didn't really have an answer. "Look, thanks for the coffee, but as I said before, I've got paperwork to do."

She looked at his desk. "Which is exactly why you need my help. A sheriff shouldn't be doing paperwork. He should be out making sure his town is safe from bad guys while his trusty assistant keeps his office running smoothly."

"Somehow I don't think you'll keep my office running smoothly." He squinted at her. "And why do you want to work for me? What happened to your store in Houston?"

"It's still there. And I plan to get back to it as soon as I earn enough money to pay Emmett to fix my car. Which should be around the same time that your assistant comes back. So you see, this is a perfect setup for both of us."

There was nothing perfect about Spring working for him. "Why doesn't Dirk just loan you the money to fix your Jeep? I think he can afford it."

Her cheeks flushed, and her eyes snapped with anger. "He can, but sometimes people are stingy. Now do I get the job or not?"

Ahh, so that was it. She and Dirk had gotten into some kind of family squabble. A squabble Waylon wanted no part of. He got to his feet. "Not." He took Spring's arm and escorted her to the door. "Thanks for the coffee, but I like mine black. No sugar. No fake flavoring."

He guided her out into the foyer before he stepped back into his office and locked the door. He released the breath he didn't even know he'd been holding before he walked over, picked up the cup of coffee, and dropped it in the trash. He needed to start on the pile of paperwork. But instead he sat down, opened his personal laptop, and looked at his online dating picture.

Spring was right. His nose did look huge. And with his day's growth of beard and sour expression, he did look like a serial killer. He glanced at the door before he picked up his phone. He smoothed back his hair, pinned on a smile, then lifted the phone above his head. The selfie wasn't any better than the first. His nose didn't look huge, but his smile looked fake as hell. He tossed his phone down and went back to work.

An hour later, he'd only finished a few of the reports he needed to get done. He rubbed at his temples. He had a bitch of a headache, no doubt from lack of caffeine. He had just decided to head over to Lucy's Place Diner for a cup of coffee when he heard Tucker's laughter. He got up and unlocked his door to find Tucker standing in front of Gail's desk, flirting with the woman sitting behind it. A woman Waylon had lost all patience with.

"What do you think you're doing?" he asked.

Tucker immediately came to attention. "I just stopped by to check in, Sheriff, and got to talking with our new assistant."

"She's not our new assistant." He glared at Spring, who started typing on the computer like she *was* the new assistant. He stepped closer and stared at the screen. "How did you get into our system?"

She stopped typing. "Tucker was nice enough to give me the password. And I was just emailing you the phone messages I took while you were locked in your office. But now that you're here." She picked up a stack of messages and read them off. "Someone broke into Miley Gaines's car and took her Garth Brooks CDs. But after talking to her, I'm pretty sure it was her ex-boyfriend. She broke up with him and he'd bought her the CDs. Glen Stafford is convinced that Dale Roberts is growing marijuana on his property. Joe Foster lost his cow. And Zane Arrington called to see if you wanted to come to dinner tonight. Carly's making her braised beef." She set down the notes. "I told him that you'd be there. I didn't think you'd want to miss out on Carly's pot roast. It's to die for."

"It sure is," Tucker agreed enthusiastically. "I stop by the diner for it every Thursday night." He paused and looked longingly at Spring. "Maybe you'd like to join me one night."

"Why, aren't you the sweetest thang." Spring flashed a bright smile that made Tucker's cheeks turn pink. "I'd love to."

Waylon didn't know why he suddenly felt so ticked off. Maybe because his wet-behind-the-ears deputy had just gotten a date while Waylon couldn't get one woman from the entire country to "hug" him.

He glared down at Spring. "You need to go." He crossed his arms and used his no-nonsense sheriff's voice. "Now. Like right this—"

The phone rang. Spring gave him a sweet-as-sugar smile before she answered it. "Sheriff Kendall's office. How can I help you?" She paused. "Oh, hi, Mrs. Daily. This is Spring Hadley . . . I'm just helping out the sheriff until Gail comes back . . . yes, Deputy Tucker told me all about her poor mama falling and breaking her hip. In fact, I just got through sending her a big bouquet of flowers from the sheriff."

Waylon opened his mouth, then snapped it

closed. He should've sent Gail's mama flowers. It annoyed him to no end that Spring had thought of it before he had.

"Sure thing. Hold on, I'll get him." Spring held out the phone. "It's Joanna Daily. She wants you to stop by and pick up some dog food for Sherlock. He ate the last of it this morning."

Waylon took the phone. "Hi, Joanna. I'll be sure to pick up a bag on my way home."

Joanna spoke in an excited voice. "I'm so pleased you hired Spring Hadley. I felt guilty not being able to help you out when you so desperately need it. But it sounds like everything worked out for the best."

He shot a glance over at Spring. "I didn't hire Spring Hadley."

"You mean that sweet girl is working for free? Now, that's not right, Waylon. Especially when the county gives you plenty of money for an assistant. Or have they? I'll call the county clerk right now and give her a piece of my mind."

Before Waylon could say a word, the phone went dead. He replaced it in the cradle before he looked at Spring. Her smile was even bigger, as if she knew she had him tarred and feathered. She picked up the cup from her desk and held it out.

"Strong, black, and unflavored."

CHAPTER SEVEN

SPRING HADN'T INTENTIONALLY SET OUT to piss off the sheriff. She just desperately needed a job. She could've asked Carly for a job at Lucy's Place Diner or Savannah for a job at Home Sweet Home, but they were both married to her cousins and she wanted to prove that she could stand on her own two feet without the help of her family. She wanted to prove that she wasn't the baby who needed to be coddled. She was a responsible, self-sufficient woman who could get her own job.

Now all she had to do was convince the sheriff.

That wasn't going to be easy. Waylon Kendall didn't like her, and he made no bones about it. After she had offered him the black coffee, he'd told her that he wanted her gone by the time he got back. Then he'd locked up his office and walked out the door. He hadn't returned.

His behavior confused her. Her ability to make friends was the one thing she was better at than her sisters. She had been the most popular triplet in high school and college. The one who always got invited to parties. The one who always had a date. Socializing came easily to her. Which explained why she sold the most inventory at the store. Granny Bon had always said that she could sell a case of bibles to the Devil himself. And if she could do that, she figured she could talk a sourpuss lawman into giving her a job. The sheriff just needed a little more time to get to know her. That was all. Once he knew her, he'd love her.

The door opened, and Emmett Daily stepped in. Spring had met him numerous times when she'd been in town before. He was Joanna Daily's husband and owned the gas station and garage where Spring's Jeep was now getting fixed. He had a pronounced limp from a war injury, kind eyes, and a friendly smile.

"Howdy, Miss Hadley," he said as he pulled off his cowboy hat. "You look mighty pretty today. Joanna used to own a yellow dress similar to the one you got on. Always made her look like a ray of sunshine. Of course, she's my sunshine whatever she wears."

The sweet comment made Spring love him even more. "Thank you, Mr. Daily. You're a ray of sunshine yourself. You certainly brightened my day."

He smiled, showing off a chipped front tooth. "Call me Emmett. Everyone does."

"And please call me Spring. What can I do for you, Emmett?"

He pulled a set of keys out of his front pocket. "I brought you your Jeep."

She was surprised. "I thought you weren't going to get to it until next week."

"That's what I planned. Since I don't have your

cousin Cole helping me anymore, I'm pretty backed up. But then Joanna called me this morning and told me about the sheriff hiring you." His eyes twinkled. "And I figured you'd need it to get to your new job."

"Thank you so much, but I'm afraid I don't have the money to pay you yet. That's one of the reasons I needed to get a job."

"No worries." He set the keys on the desk. "Just pay me when you can. The entire town appreciates you helping the sheriff out while Gail is gone to take care of her mama."

The entire town already thought she was working for the sheriff? She'd forgotten how quickly news traveled in a small town. And maybe that would work in her favor. If she could get the entire town to accept her as the sheriff's assistant it might be harder for him to get rid of her.

"I look forward to helping the sheriff out. He certainly seems to be overworked."

Emmett shook his head. "Waylon has put most of the pressure on himself."

"Why do you think that is?" Spring leaned in, wanting to hear more about the sheriff. But just then the phone rang, and Emmett tipped his hat and headed for the door.

"I'll let you get back to work."

"Thank you for bringing back my car," she said before answering the phone. "Sheriff Kendall's office. How can I help you?"

"You can quit screwing around and get your ass back home!"

Summer's loud voice had Spring's butt lifting off the chair. Once her butt resettled, she yelled right back. "I'm not screwing around! And I'm not coming home. Especially when my sister thinks I'm a ditz."

"You are a ditz. Only a ditz would forget to—"

Autumn's soothing voice cut off Summer's screech. "You are not a ditz, Spring. It was an accident. One that Summer and I both know you're sorry about. And Summer is sorry she got so upset and hurt your feelings."

In the background, Spring could hear Summer's denial. "No, I'm not sorry. She needs to pull her head out of her—hey, stop pushing me." A door slammed shut, and Autumn came back on.

"Sweetie, you need to come home. We miss you, and we can't run Seasons without you. All your regular customers have been asking about you."

The sadness Spring had been trying to ignore since leaving Houston welled up inside her. "I miss you too. Although I don't miss Summer."

"That's not true, Spring. You miss Summer as much as she misses you. You're just hurt. And Summer is just stressed about losing the store. Come back and I promise we'll get everything worked out. Dirk told me about your Jeep, and I'm more than happy to send you the money to fix it."

It was surprising how much she wanted to go back to Houston. Back to the security and comfort of being part of the Hadley triplets. But there was another part of her that had started to wonder if Granny Bon was right. Was she living her dream or was she living Summer's? And maybe a few weeks away from her sisters would help her figure that out.

"I can't come back, Audie."

"What? Is this about getting back at Summer for being so mean?"

"When I first ran off, it was. I wanted to make Summer pay for yelling at me. But then I realized that she was right. Leaving the store open was an irresponsible thing to do." She paused. "Even Granny Bon and Dirk think so."

"You're not irresponsible. You're free-spirited." Autumn paused. "Granny Bon called and gave Summer and me the same lecture she gave you about us all needing time apart. But she's wrong. We're not just sisters. We're triplets. We started out as one before we split into three. Because of that, we have a special bond that Granny can't understand. Things don't feel right when we're separated. Even Summer feels it. Which is why she's been acting like a caged animal."

Tears sprang to Spring's eyes, but she blinked them back. "I know. I miss you too. But maybe Granny is right. Maybe we do need a little time away from each other to figure out who we are separately. I'm not talking forever. Just a few months."

There was a long pause before Autumn spoke. "You need to do what you feel is right. Although Summer isn't going to like it. Not only does she miss you, she's also worried about the store. Our sales so far this year have been dismal. And with you gone, they'll only get worse. Summer's temperament isn't exactly suited for retail. And while I'm more patient, I didn't inherit your and Dirk's charm either. You are great with people."

The words soothed Spring's bruised ego. "Thanks, Audie. But I don't know if my salesmanship is going to make a difference. I talked with

Dirk, and he agrees with you. He thinks the store will eventually fail, and we should jump ship now before we get too far into debt."

Autumn sighed. "Now all we need to do is convince Summer."

"We'll do it when I get back. With Dirk, we own three-fourth of the business. Majority rules."

"Somehow I don't think that's the way Summer will see it, but enough depressing talk. Tell me about your new job."

Spring finally realized that she was talking on the phone at the sheriff's office. "How did you know to call me here?"

"When Summer couldn't get you, she called Dirk. He said your cellphone was broken, but he'd just talked to Joanna Daily and she'd told him that you'd gotten a job with the sheriff. Is this the same hot sheriff that was at Dirk and Gracie's wedding?"

"As a matter of fact, it is."

"Now I understand why you don't want to come home," Autumn teased.

"He might be hot, but he's also a little too uptight for me. And just for the record, he didn't exactly hire me." She proceeded to fill her sister in on all the details. When she was finished, Autumn laughed.

"The poor man doesn't know the whirlwind he's up against. When you want something, you're almost as tenacious as Summer. Now tell me about my cute nieces."

Spring only got to tell her sister a few stories about Luana, Lucinda, and Luella before a customer came into Seasons and Autumn had to go wait on her. After Spring placed the phone in the cradle, she glanced at the clock and realized it was almost four o'clock. Figuring that was a good quitting time, she closed down her computer. Since it didn't look like the sheriff was coming back, she decided to lock the front doors. Tucker had shown her the filing cabinet drawer where the keys were kept. But once she had them in hand, she didn't lock the front doors.

Instead, she glanced at the locked door of the sheriff's office.

When she had been in his office earlier, she hadn't taken time to look around. She'd been too busy trying to get a job. And then there had been the entire online dating thing. Why would the sheriff need to join an online dating site? Men as young and good-looking as he was shouldn't have a problem getting a date. Unless he had a flaw she wasn't aware of. It certainly wasn't his body or looks.

It only took trying a few keys before she found the one that unlocked the door to his office. Once inside, she strolled around the room, checking out the map of the county hanging on one wall and the pictures of previous sheriffs hanging on the other. The last sheriff shared Sheriff Kendall's features and rusty brown hair. She studied the somber face of Malcolm Kendall, wondering if it was his father or an uncle.

Next to the pictures was some kind of sheriff's oath. Spring bypassed it and moved to the desk. The chair was high-backed and leather and held the indentation of the sheriff's butt. He had a nice butt. It filled out the pockets of his Wranglers just enough to make a woman want to slide her hands over the firm buns and squeeze. She laughed at the thought of his reaction if she ever did that.

She sat down in the chair. His desk was neat and tidy. Maybe a little too neat and tidy. Everything seemed to be placed around the desk calendar like the face of a clock. The computer was at twelve o'clock. The phone at two. A pen was lined up perfectly at four. Pad of paper at six. Stapler at eight. A family photograph at ten.

She leaned in and looked at the picture. Malcolm Kendall sat next to a pretty woman with blond hair and green eyes. They were surrounded by their family. Two young couples, three children, and Waylon. He was smiling brighter than she'd ever seen him smile. It was obvious that being with family made him happy. And maybe that explained why he'd joined an online dating site. He was ready for a family of his own.

The only thing out of place in the weird clock arrangement on the desk was a book that sat next to the picture. Curious about the sheriff's reading tastes, she picked it up and leafed through it. It was a self-help book on becoming a leader. She found highlighted passages about gaining respect, commanding authority, and dealing with the pressures of being the boss.

For the first time since she'd met the sheriff, she saw him as a human being instead of a robotic lawman. It appeared that he had insecurities just like everyone else. She flipped through the pages taking note of the numerous highlighted passages. A lot of insecurities. She glanced at the sheriff's oath that hung on the wall and read it. It was a long and intimidating list.

She'd thought she had a lot of responsibilities at

her store. It was nothing compared to the responsibility of taking care of an entire town. The sheriff didn't have to deal with indecisive customers and late shipments. He had to make sure the people in his town were safe and protected. And in order to do that, they had to trust him completely. They had to know he was a strong leader and a tough lawman who believed in and followed the laws of the land.

Empathy welled up inside her. Poor Waylon. No wonder he didn't smile. Taking care of an entire town was a huge burden. A burden he had to deal with alone. He couldn't exactly sit down at the diner and tell people he was struggling under the weight of his job. That wouldn't make people feel confident.

Was that the reason he'd joined an online dating site? It made sense. He needed someone to talk to. Someone who didn't live in the town. Someone who wouldn't spread gossip and rumors about the sheriff.

She glanced at the computer, and a thought struck her. Maybe she could help Waylon with more than just office work. Maybe she could help him find someone to confide in. Someone who could make him smile as brightly as when he was with his family. With the tough lawman persona he'd built around himself, it would be a challenge. But Spring had always loved challenges.

And she was a sucker for a happy ending.

CHAPTER EIGHT

ZANE AND CARLY ARRINGTON'S EAR-HART Ranch was one of the biggest spreads in the county. It had acres and acres of prime land, plenty of cattle to graze it, and a beautiful stone ranch house with a wraparound porch. Waylon pulled his truck up to the porch and hopped out. Sherlock climbed down from the truck at a slower speed. Although he perked up a little when Zane's herding dog came racing out of the barn to greet him.

"Hey, Shep," Waylon said as he gave the dog's ears a good scratch. "See if you can't give Sherlock a few lessons on herding cows while you two are playing." If Sherlock wouldn't hunt, maybe he would herd. But his dog didn't seem to be in much of a hurry to do anything but follow Waylon up on the porch steps and plop down by a rocker.

Waylon rolled his eyes just as Zane threw open the door. "Hey, Way! I'm glad you decided to come." He held the door. When Waylon was inside, he yelled to the dogs. "You and Sherlock coming in, Shep?" The dogs must've declined because Zane closed the door and turned to Waylon. "Come on back to my study. Carly isn't quite through with dinner, and she gets mad if I sneak tastes while she's cooking."

"I guess the Sanders sisters are covering for her at the diner tonight," Waylon said as he followed Zane.

"They've taken over cooking every night. Carly has been a little tired lately."

As Waylon walked past him into the study, he took note of Zane's worried expression. "Everything okay?"

"She says she's just been working too hard, but I talked her into making an appointment with a doctor next week just to be sure." Zane walked to the mini-bar. "You want something to drink?"

Waylon moved to the fireplace where a fire was blazing. It had been a warm few days, but it was still February and the nights got chilly. "Just a Dr Pepper for me."

Zane glanced over. "It's okay to have a drink every now and then, Way. You're off-duty."

Waylon wished he could be off-duty. He sat down in a chair that flanked the fireplace. "I need to check on Jonas after dinner. He's been falling asleep on the job."

Zane grabbed two Dr Peppers from the mini fridge and handed one to Waylon before he sat down. "Well, that's not good. Have you thought of a way to talk him into retiring?"

Waylon shook his head as he popped the top of the soda can. "I don't know what he'd do if he didn't have the job to go to. I told him Tucker would take nights, but he said he wanted nights. I think nights are when he's the loneliest."

Zane crossed his boots up on the ottoman and blew out his breath. "Damn. Losing your wife has to be tough. I don't know what I'd do without Carly." He glanced over at Waylon. "What about his kids? Maybe you could mention something to them, and they could suggest he moves closer to the grandkids."

"They both offered, but Jonas refuses. I think he isn't ready to leave the house he shared with his wife. Or her gravesite."

Zane sipped his Dr Pepper for a few minutes before he spoke. "Maybe he should try online dating. I hear anyone can get a date using those sites."

The sip Waylon had just taken went down wrong, and he choked.

Zane jumped up and thumped him on the back. "You've really become a teetotaler if DP is too strong for you."

Carly appeared in the doorway. "Is everything okay? Do I need to call an ambulance or perform the Heimlich?"

Waylon drew in a ragged breath and cleared his throat. "I'm fine. My soda just went down wrong. Thanks for inviting me to dinner, Carly. The smell of your braised beef already has my stomach growling."

"You're welcome. The dinner rolls just need to finish browning, and then we can eat." She waited for Zane to sit down, then sat on the arm of his chair and took his can of Dr Pepper. Waylon had always envied their relationship. They seemed completely comfortable with one another. Like they'd known each other all their lives instead of less than two

years. She took a sip of pop and handed the can
back to Zane. "So how have you been, Waylon?"

"Busy."

"I know how that goes, but I'm sure things will
slow down now that you found someone to help
you out. I couldn't keep the diner open if not for
the Sanders sisters. And I'm glad that you hired
Spring. She's so friendly and vivacious."

Vivacious wasn't the word. Tenacious was more
like it. He'd had to get downright mean to get it
through her head that he wasn't hiring her. He
didn't need a vivacious young woman working in
his office. He needed someone like Gail. Someone
who went about their work without putting their
cute little nose in his personal business.

"I didn't hire Spring," he said.

Carly looked confused. "But she answered your
phone?"

Since his mama had taught him to never talk
badly about a lady, he didn't go into detail about
the arrogant, annoying way she'd tried to ramrod
him for a job. "There was a little misunderstanding,
but it's cleared up now." When he'd stopped by the
office to lock up, there was no smiling daffodil in
sight. But his feeling of satisfaction was short lived
when Zane exchanged looks with Carly.

"I don't think it's completely cleared up, Way,"
Zane said.

A prickle of apprehension tiptoed up Waylon's
spine. "What do you mean?"

"The entire town is talking about how wonderful it is that Spring Hadley is helping out while
Gail is gone."

His shoulders relaxed. "They'll figure it out

soon enough. People are always getting their wires crossed about something."

"They're not the only ones who got their wires crossed. I was talking with Dirk right before you got here, and he told me to tell you thanks for giving his sister a job. He said that she needed a little ego boost. I guess Dirk cooked her a special dinner tonight to celebrate her new job."

Waylon suddenly felt like a fish that had just swallowed a hook whole. It was one thing for the town to think Spring was working for him and another for Dirk Hadley to think it. He was one of the most respected citizens in Bliss. The money he'd invested in the town had helped with its revitalization and people were talking about electing him the next mayor. How was Waylon going to tell Dirk that he hadn't hired his sister? Of course, maybe he wouldn't have to tell him. Maybe Spring was telling him right at that very moment. And if that was the case, then he better head over there and try to smooth things over.

He got to his feet. "I'm sorry, but I'm going to have to take a rain check on dinner."

Carly and Zane exchanged another look before Zane stood. "Sure thing, Way. We'll make it another night."

"I'll pack you up some dinner to go," Carly said.

Since Dirk had built his and Gracie's house on Arrington land, it didn't take Waylon long to get there. The house was a large two-story home that looked like it belonged in a rich neighborhood in Austin rather than smack dab in the middle of Arrington cow country. The five garage doors were made of rich, dark oak that matched the wooden doors of the barn. Waylon pulled up in the circular drive and cut the engine.

On the way over, he'd tried to figure out how to get out of this mess. But he hadn't come up with one single solution . . . other than giving Spring a job as his assistant. Just the thought had the muscles in his neck tightening. He had enough to worry about with Jonas and Tucker. He didn't need another employee who needed to be babysat. And Spring would need to be babysat. Not only was she nosy, she was a loose cannon. There was no telling what she would do or say at any given moment.

She was also messy and disorganized. Gail kept her desk neat and orderly. By the time Waylon got back to the office, Gail's desk looked like it had been hit by a cyclone. Empty Diet Coke cans, candy bar and chip wrappers were intermingled with message memos that held a scribbled language he couldn't decipher. Each unreadable message was surrounded by a chain of daisy doodles. Considering Spring's many faults, surely Dirk wouldn't blame Waylon for not hiring her.

He opened his truck door and hopped out. Dirk and Gracie loved animals, but he decided to leave Sherlock sleeping in the front seat. He did, however, move the container of braised beef Carly had given him to the bed of the truck. Food had always trumped sleep with Sherlock.

Once Waylon was standing on the front porch, he had second thoughts about Dirk understanding why he couldn't hire his sister. Dirk loved his sisters and probably didn't see their faults. Which meant that Waylon might not get a warm welcome. He could only hope that Dirk wasn't the type who threw a punch before he listened to reason. But Dirk didn't look ticked when he opened the door. He wore the same easygoing smile he always did.

"Well, speak of the devil. We were just talking about you."

Waylon took off his hat. "Hey, Dirk." He smiled at the baby Dirk held. "Hey, Luana."

Dirk looked a little confused. "How did you know this was Luana? Everyone but family has trouble telling the girls apart."

"She has that cute dimple in her cheek." He cleared his throat. "So I guess Spring told you about what happened this—"

Gracie appeared, holding Lucinda and Luella, and cut him off. "Hi, Waylon." Waylon had grown up with Gracie and her cousin Becky. They were two of the few women he felt completely comfortable around. She stepped out on the porch and gave him a kiss on the cheek. "Come on in. I'm sure you're already stuffed with Carly's braised beef, but we've got apple pie for dessert. And Dirk's apple pie almost beats Ms. Marble's."

Dirk flashed a smile. "Why, thank you, honey." He tucked an arm around her and gave her a quick kiss before he turned his smile on Waylon. "And I owe you more than a slice of apple pie. Thanks, Way. I sure appreciate what you did for Spring. She's thrilled with her new job."

All Waylon could do was stand there feeling like a real heel. Obviously, Spring had more than a few screws loose. He'd made it perfectly clear that she didn't have a job. But maybe she'd been too embarrassed to tell her brother after he'd made her a big celebration dinner. Waylon understood.

It would be hard to set things straight with Dirk, Gracie, and three cute little babies smiling back at you. He certainly couldn't do it.

"Thank you for the offer of pie," he said. "But I was wondering if I could have a word with Spring?"

"She's not here," Dirk said. "She insisted on staying in that trailer of hers. No doubt because she's still a little mad at me."

"She's not mad at you," Gracie said. "She just wants to prove to everyone that she can make it on her own."

"Spring does not do things on her own. I give her one night," Dirk said. "Once she discovers she can't take hour-long showers, she'll be back."

"I wouldn't be too sure about that. I think your sister is more determined than she looks."

Stubborn was more like it.

"Where's her trailer?" Waylon asked. He hadn't seen it when he pulled up.

"She moved it a couple miles up the road to the acreage the Arringtons gave to my sisters. Which is another reason she'll be back. She's never slept out in the country in her life. She doesn't realize how dark and isolated it can feel." Dirk suddenly looked concerned. "In fact, maybe I'd better go check on her."

"I'll check on her," Waylon said as he pulled on his hat. "I'll give you a call after I make sure she's okay." Once he talked with Spring, he'd need to explain things to Dirk. Hopefully, he would understand.

It wasn't hard to find the trailer. With light pouring from every tiny window, it shone like a pink beacon in the moonless night. Waylon parked on the road and got out. Sherlock must've had to take a leak because he jumped down and followed Waylon through the tall winter grass to the trailer, stopping to mark his territory every few feet.

Right before they reached the front door, a movement in the juniper trees caught his attention. Normally, Waylon wouldn't have paid it much mind. There were all kinds of wild critters roaming the Arrington land from deer to armadillos. But Joe Foster's cow was still missing, and he wanted to make sure it hadn't somehow found its way onto Arrington land. He instructed Sherlock to sit and stay, then moved slowly toward the trees. If it was the cow, he didn't want to startle it and send it running into the next county.

He came around the trees just in time to see a mule deer bounce away. He was about to head back to Spring's trailer when a quick movement in his peripheral vision caused him to instinctively whirl around and throw up an arm to fend off the object coming toward him. Something hit his forearm before he knocked it out of his assailant's hand. He would have wrestled the attacker to the ground if not for the feminine cry of pain.

He relaxed his defensive posture. "Spring?" A groan of either pain or annoyance was his only answer. He squinted at her shadowy form. "Are you okay?"

"No. I think you broke my wrist."

He wanted to ask her what the hell she'd been doing, but his concern had him shelving the question and carefully guiding Spring back to the trailer. The door stood wide open as if she'd raced out of it. He helped her up the steps.

The inside of the trailer was as messy as the last time he'd been there. He moved the yellow dress and a shoe off the bench seat of the little dining booth and guided her down to it.

She wore a pink nightshirt with "Sleep Happy" written across the front in rainbow letters. And it was obvious by the two stiff peaks poking through the thin material that she wasn't wearing a bra. He tried to ignore this fact as he crouched in front of her. "Let me see your wrist."

She continued to cradle her hand. "Would you like to explain what you were doing sneaking around my trailer, Sheriff?"

"I wasn't sneaking." He stopped when he realized that was exactly what he had been doing. "Okay, I was sneaking, but only to catch a cow."

"You came out here looking for a missing cow?"

"No, I came out here to make sure you understood that I'm not hiring you." He held out his hand. "Now let me see your wrist."

"It's okay. It just stings a little." When he continued to hold out his hand, she heaved a sigh and rested her hand in his. Her skin was soft, her fingers long with closely trimmed nails that were painted a bright yellow with daisies on the thumbnail. When he didn't see any marks, he turned her hand over. A red welt marred the smooth pale skin of her wrist. The sight made him cringe. He'd never hurt a woman in his life. Not even Cheryl Lee Denson when she'd gotten plastered on mulberry wine and tried to body slam him for refusing to let her drive drunk.

He gently ran his thumb back and forth over the

red mark. "I'm sorry. I didn't mean to hurt you. I just reacted."

"It was my fault. I should've looked closer before I swung."

He continued to rub her wrist. He couldn't seem to stop. "What did you hit me with, anyway?"

"The non-stick aluminum skillet Autumn got me last year for Christmas."

"I hate to point this out, but you can't knock a man out with an aluminum skillet. It needs to be cast iron."

She blew her bangs out of her eyes and sent him an exasperated look. "I think I figured that out."

He couldn't help but smile. The woman was annoying, but she was also pretty darned cute. Still, he needed to remain firm if he wanted to get things straight between them. "You figured that out, but you can't seem to figure out that I'm not hiring you to fill in for Gail."

She tipped her head and studied him. "And why is that exactly?"

He reached over and pulled the heart-printed dishtowel off the oven handle, then he opened the mini-fridge and took out the tiniest ice cube tray from the tiniest freezer he'd ever seen in his life. He popped the small cubes into the towel, then held the towel against her wrist before he answered her question.

"You have no experience working for a sheriff's department. You work in retail."

"True, but I can answer phones and take messages. That's more than you have now."

She had a point. One he wasn't about to concede. He did not want to work with Spring, and he didn't need to explain why. "I've been doing just fine," he said.

"That's hogwash and you know it. I must've taken thirty calls today."

"Thirty? You only took around ten messages."

"Because half of the calls weren't things a sheriff needs to deal with—like Mrs. Miller calling to report that all the neighborhood cats need to be neutered."

He shook his head. "Mrs. Miller calls three times a day about something. Cats needing neutered, dogs pooping on her lawn, a dead pigeon that hit her front window."

"I think she just needs someone to talk to. Her family has all moved away."

"I run a sheriff's office, not a counseling center."

"I don't mind talking with her, Waylon."

It was the first time she'd used his name without his title, and the sound of it coming from her lips was distracting. As were the twilight-blue eyes that stared back at him from only inches away. For a second, he forgot what they were talking about, and he had to shake his head to clear it. "You're not working for me."

She studied him long and hard before a smile broke over her face. "This isn't about me not having experience, is it?" She sent him a knowing look. "You're hot for me, Sheriff. And you're afraid that if I work in your office, you won't be able to resist me."

CHAPTER NINE

THE SHERIFF LOOKED LIKE SPRING had hit him over the head with a cast iron skillet. He was still crouched in front of her, and at her words, he fell on his butt and banged his head on the pantry door. She bit back a smile. She didn't know why she enjoyed teasing the man so much. Maybe because he was so straight-laced.

She held out the dishtowel of ice. "Here. You need this more than I do." He didn't acknowledge the ice. He just stared at her as if she was some kind of alien from another planet.

She smiled. "You can't tell me that you haven't noticed the sexual chemistry between us." He opened his mouth, but nothing came out so she continued. "It's no big deal. I'm sure I'm not the only woman who you've been attracted to. And you certainly aren't the first man to light my pilot light. But just because you find someone hot, doesn't mean you have to go to bed with them."

He blinked those pretty green eyes, but still couldn't seem to speak. And that was probably a good thing. It would give her plenty of time to convince him she was the right girl for the job.

Because after the celebratory dinner Dirk made her and the congratulatory phone call from Granny Bon, she wasn't about to go back and tell her family that she hadn't really gotten the job. She was going to get this job. And she was going to be the best darn assistant the sheriff had ever had.

"I mean it's not like we're randy fifteen-year-olds, Waylon," she said. "Is it okay if I call you Waylon? Sheriff Kendall just seems a little weird when we're going to be working together. Anyway, we're both old enough to realize that there is more to a relationship than sex. No matter how great someone is in bed, it's the time out of bed that really counts. And you and I are not a good match. We're two completely different people. I'm an extrovert. You're an introvert. I love people. You seem to hate them. I'm a big city girl and you're satisfied living in a small little town trying to prove that you're a good sheriff."

He finally found his voice. "Excuse me?"

She cleared her throat. "I mean you're satisfied living in a small town and being a good sheriff." She moved on. "And knowing that we're complete opposites, there's no way we're going to let a little sexual chemistry get us to do something that we'll regret later. So you have nothing to worry about. Even if you wanted to boink me on your desk, I wouldn't let you. Your honor is safe with me."

He choked, and his eyes bugged out. Even bugged, they were beautiful. The prettiest green she'd ever seen. They went perfectly with his sun-streaked brown hair that was mussed and sexy.

He cleared his throat. "My honor is safe because

I have no desire to boink you over my desk."

"I didn't say over. I said on. Which only confirms that you *have* been having naughty thoughts about me, Waylon." She needed to stop with the teasing, but damn it was hard when he was such an easy target.

"Sheriff Kendall," he growled. He used the table to pull himself to his feet. "And I have not been having naughty thoughts about you. The reason I'm not hiring you is because you annoy me. You're too blunt. You're too messy. You're too nosy. And you're too . . ." he looked at her yellow dress flung over the table, ". . .bright!"

He turned for the door. Luckily, the door handle was tricky, and he couldn't get it opened. Which gave Spring a few seconds to come up with another plan. Sometimes having overactive tear ducts came in handy.

She blinked some tears into her eyes before she spoke in a soft voice. "You're right. I am too blunt. And messy. And nosy. Even my own sister hates me." She sniffed.

He slowly turned. "You can stop anytime. I'm not going to fall for a few tears." But he was already falling. She could see it in his terrified eyes. "I'm sure your sister loves you."

"I don't know about that." More tears filled her eyes, and these she didn't have to force. "Summer has always found fault with me. She thinks I'm a real ditz who is immature and irresponsible. And come to find out, the rest of my family feels the same way. Everyone thinks I'm not smart enough to take care of myself." A tear rolled down her cheek, but she quickly brushed it away. "And they might be right. I can't remember important things, or manage money, or even choose the right pan to use as a weapon. I'm pretty much a failure at everything I do. You're right not to want to hire me."

Waylon stared at her for only a second before he blew out a long sigh. He held up a finger. "One week. We'll try it for one week. But if you screw up once—I mean *one time*—you're gone. No excuses, no tears, and no begging." He pulled a bandana from his back pocket and handed it to her.

She ignored it and jumped up to give him a big hug. Because if anyone needed a hug it was the sheriff. "Thank you! I promise you won't regret it. I'm going to be the best sheriff's helper in the entire state of Texas." She stepped back. "Make that the entire country. I'm going to be efficient and hardworking. And if you don't like my work, I'll leave without one little ol' word."

His eyebrows lifted. "Somehow I doubt that."

"You're right. I'll say, 'Goodbye, Sheriff Kendall. I appreciate the opportunity to prove my worth.'"

"Waylon. If we're going to be working together, you can call me Waylon."

She shook her head. "You were right before. It's best if we keep things on a professional level. I'll call you Sheriff Kendall and you can call me Miss Hadley."

He nodded. "All right, Miss Hadley. I'll expect to see you at seven thirty tomorrow morning."

She tried not to cringe at the early hour. Seven thirty? That would mean she'd have to get up at six thirty to get ready. And the only time she'd been up at six thirty in the morning was when she and her sisters had gone to Vegas and stayed out all night partying.

But she plastered on a bright smile. "Seven thirty sharp."

He nodded before he turned to the door, but he still couldn't get the handle to work. She squeezed around him and gave it a little jiggle before pushing it open. "It's a little temperamental." She flashed him a smile. "But I'm good with temperamental things."

"Are you calling me temperamental, Miss Hadley?"

With him standing so close, the spark of sexual attraction flared again and settled in a warm flame deep inside her stomach. "If the shoe fits, Sheriff Kendall," she said in a husky voice that must've betrayed that warm flame.

Waylon's eyes darkened, and his nostrils flared as if he was a stallion that had just caught her scent. They both stilled; not even a breath fell from their lips as the flame inside Spring grew higher and brighter. Then he blinked.

"Goodnight, Miss Hadley."

"Goodnight, Sheriff Kendall." She placed a hand on her trembling tummy as he stepped down from the trailer and walked away. Instead of closing the door, she stood there for a few moments leaning against the wall of the kitchenette and wondering what it was about Waylon that made her libido go wacky.

It wacked out again when Waylon peeked his head back in. He was wearing his cowboy hat and holding out her skillet. "Next time you find someone sneaking around your trailer, lock the doors and call the sheriff."

She took the pan. "I would've, but someone broke my cellphone, and I can't get a new one until I get my first check. Which brings up a good question? What is my salary?"

"We'll discuss it if you show up on time tomorrow." He turned and walked away.

She moved to the doorway and called to him. "I'll show up on time. Don't you worry." When he and his dog had almost disappeared, she glanced around at the dark, spooky night. "Are there any wild animals I need to be aware of?"

He stopped and turned. "If you're scared, maybe you should stay with your brother."

She tipped up her chin. "I'm not scared. I was just asking a question."

"There are no lions, or tigers, or bears. But to put your mind at ease, I'll have my deputy Jonas drive by in a couple hours just to make sure everything is okay."

It was a sweet gesture. One she wasn't about to decline. She was a little scared being alone. Or maybe more than a little. "Thank you."

He tipped his hat before he walked away.

She stood in the doorway and watched his nice butt in his tight Wranglers disappear into the darkness before she closed the door. Surprisingly, she didn't feel as scared anymore. Maybe because her fear of being alone was eclipsed by her fear that if Waylon ever wanted to boink her on his desk, she might just let him.

She was so worried about being late for her first day, she got very little sleep that night. She finally got up around five thirty and got ready, hoping to impress the sheriff by being early. Showering in her trailer's itty-bitty shower was a challenge. It was no more than a small bench and a handheld nozzle that had the water pressure of a drippy faucet. But she managed.

Since the sheriff didn't like bright, she went with her most subdued outfit—a light peach V-necked sweater, white pencil skirt, and tan cowboy boots with peach heart inlays. She was so proud of herself for being ready an hour before she had to be to work, she decided she had time to make herself some tea. She was putting the teakettle on her two-burner stove, when she peeked out her window and saw a sheriff's car parked in the road. Not Waylon's SUV, but a four-door sedan. She walked outside to thank the deputy for checking up on her and was surprised to find an older gentleman sound asleep behind the wheel. Worried that he wasn't just asleep, she gently shook his shoulder.

"Excuse me, sir. Are you okay?"

His eyes popped open. "Huh . . . what?"

"I'm sorry to wake you." She held out a hand. "I'm Spring Hadley, Sheriff Kendall's new assistant."

"You didn't wake me. I was just resting my eyes." He straightened, and then cringed and grabbed his neck.

"Oh, no, did you hurt your neck?"

"It's just a crick. I'll be fine." But he didn't look fine. He held his head at an odd angle, and his features were scrunched in pain. As much as she was on a schedule, she couldn't ignore his discomfort.

She opened his door. "Come into the trailer and we'll put some heat on it."

Jonas was as stubborn as an old mule to begin with. But after Spring applied the towel she'd warmed in the microwave to his neck and made him a cup of tea, he finally loosened up and started talking. Spring soon realized he was a sweet man who was still grieving the loss of his wife. She sat and listened sympathetically as he talked about his wife and the perfect life they'd had together before she died. It wasn't until he glanced at his watch and said he needed to get back to work that she remembered her new job.

After Jonas left, she only had thirty minutes to get to work. She made it to town in under twenty, then stopped by the diner to grab the sheriff a quick cup of coffee. But when she walked into the diner, there seemed to be some kind of disturbance. People were crowded around the counter complaining about bad service. One of the Sanders sisters, Spring didn't know which one, was standing behind the counter yelling back.

"Don't blame me. I just sling the hash. I didn't sign up to serve it too!" She took off her apron and tossed it down on the counter before she disappeared into the kitchen.

Spring's first instinct was to skip the coffee and head to the sheriff's station. But she couldn't do that. This was Carly's diner, and Carly was family. Granny Bon had always taught her that family watched out for family.

She pushed her way through the crowd until she was standing behind the counter. She smiled brightly at the angry faces. "Good morning, y'all! What seems to be the problem?"

"Food is the problem," someone yelled from the

back. "I've been here for a half hour and haven't even gotten a glass of water."

"My eggs were stone cold by the time they got to my table," someone else yelled.

A woman moved up in the crowd. "I ordered sausage and got bacon. And it wasn't even extra crispy like I like it."

"Nothing worse than limp bacon," Spring said. "But I'm sure it was just a simple mistake." She glanced around. "And haven't we all made mistakes before? I know I've made more than my fair share. Thankfully, people have forgiven me." Most people. Summer was the exception to the rule. "My Granny Bon always says that forgiveness is a gift we should all give freely."

The faces around her grew less angry, and a few smiles appeared. The woman who had pushed through the crowd nodded her head. "You're right, honey. Don't worry about my bacon. It's not the first limp thing I've had to deal with." She moved back to her booth. The other people seemed to take her lead. Spring heaved a sigh of relief and headed into the kitchen to find Carly and figure out what was going on.

But Carly wasn't in the kitchen. Only the Sanders sister who was flipping pancakes at the stove and cussing a blue streak and a busboy who was standing in the corner holding his tub of dirty dishes and looking scared.

"Where's Carly?" Spring asked the boy.

He pointed a finger at the back door. Outside, Spring found Carly leaning against the building. She was a petite woman with short blond hair and big brown eyes that made her look like a cute pixie.

But beneath the pixie features was a steely strength that Spring had always envied. Although she didn't look so strong now. Her face was pale and drawn, and she looked like she was ready to drop.

"Are you sick, Carly?" Spring asked.

Carly held a hand to her stomach. "Sort of. I haven't been feeling well. And I took a home pregnancy test last night and it came back positive."

"That's wonderful!" Spring walked over and gave her a big hug. "Congratulations!"

Carly smiled weakly. "It is wonderful news except for the fact that I'm a chef. A chef who can't stand the smell of eggs cooking."

"Uh oh."

"Exactly. And to add to it, Bella Sanders came down with a cold, my breakfast and lunch waitress quit on me this morning and my dinner waiter has decided to try out for the high school baseball team so he won't be able to show up until six."

"Well, that explains the mutiny that's taking place inside."

Carly took a deep breath. "I don't have time for this. I have to go help Stella." She headed to the door and pulled it open, but as soon as the waft of cooking scents hit her, she gagged and turned away.

"You can't go in there," Spring said. "You'll end up throwing up on someone's omelet." She could think of only one way to solve the problem. A solution that would no doubt get her fired as the sheriff's assistant. But there was no help for it. She couldn't leave her pregnant cousin-in-law in the lurch. "I'll help."

Carly didn't look too happy about the offer. In fact, she looked more than a little skeptical. No doubt she'd been talking to Spring's family and thought Spring couldn't even handle tying her shoes. "But do you know anything about waitressing?"

"Of course. I waitressed in college." It was just a little fib. She'd worked behind the counter of a coffee shop for one day. The next day she got fired for chatting too much with the customers. But she couldn't let Carly know that. She had enough to worry about. "Go on home. Stella and I will handle things from here."

Before Carly could argue, Spring headed back inside and grabbed an apron.

CHAPTER TEN

WAYLON GLANCED AT THE CLOCK on his computer and was just plain dumbstruck. He'd figured Spring would be late, but he hadn't figured she'd be over two hours late. It was already close to ten o'clock and there was no sign of her. He should be thrilled. Now he had an excuse for not hiring her that no one, not even her brother, could argue with.

But for some reason, he wasn't all that thrilled. In fact, he was a little disappointed. And he couldn't put his finger on the reason why. Maybe because she had disrupted the monotony of his everyday life. She was unpredictable and a troublemaker, but she was also kind of funny. She made him laugh, and it had been a long time since he'd found something to laugh about. Of course, he hadn't found her bizarre theory about him being sexually attracted to her amusing.

Probably because he *was* sexually attracted to her.

But it had nothing to do with Spring and everything to do with the dry spell he'd been going through since becoming sheriff. He needed sexual release, and he needed it in a bad way.

The thought had him opening his laptop and pulling up the online dating site. His eyes widened when he saw the staggering number of "hugs" he'd received on his profile page. Obviously, it just took some time for women to find you on the site. At least that's what he thought until he glanced over at his profile picture. It was a completely different picture than the one he'd taken and extremely familiar. He glanced at the picture of him with his family on the desk. The profile picture was the same picture, minus his family. How had it gotten cropped and ended up on the dating site?

It didn't take long to come up with an answer.

Spring.

It wouldn't have been hard for her to scan the picture on the printer, and then crop it and put it on his profile page. His username and passcode were stored in his laptop.

The picture wasn't the only thing she'd changed. She'd also fixed his answers on the questionnaire. He no longer had a pet peeve. His favorite movie was still *Robocop*, but now he also loved *When Harry Met Sally* and *Sabrina*. What was *Sabrina*? And his favorite authors were still Grisham and Crichton, but he also loved *Alice in Wonderland*.

He jumped up and grabbed his hat. He was going to kill her. Or at least read her the riot act. He slammed out of his office and sailed out the front door. He had just climbed in his SUV when he spotted Spring's white Jeep parked in front of the diner. The fact that she'd been having breakfast when she was supposed to be working pissed him off even more.

He got back out of his truck and headed for the diner. He couldn't give her hell in front of the townsfolk, but he could certainly drag her butt out back and do it. He stepped into the diner expecting to see her sitting at the counter or in a booth chatting it up with one of her cousins. Instead, she was hustling around with a pot of coffee filling people's cups. She was smiling brightly, but she looked frazzled. Her hair was mussed and the apron she wore was stained.

He froze in his tracks, unsure of what was going on. Had she decided to work for Carly instead of him? It seemed that way when she glanced up and saw him. Her smile faded, and a resigned look came over her face. She moved behind the counter and grabbed a to-go cup and filled it with coffee, then put the carafe back in the machine and walked over to him. "Black, no fake flavoring or sugar." When he took the cup, she sighed. "I know. I'm fired."

The words completed deflated the rant he had been about to launch into. Suddenly, he realized that he'd been looking forward to their confrontation. Which might explain his disappointment when she didn't show up for work. He liked verbally fencing with her. She was the only person who dared to stand up to the strict lawman he'd become. But she wasn't standing up to him now. She looked tired and defeated.

"So did you want to see a menu?" she asked. "Or do you just want takeout?"

He took off his hat. "I want to know what you're doing here. I thought you wanted to work for me."

"I do want to work for you. And I planned to be

at your office bright and early this morning. But when I walked in here to get your coffee—"

Mrs. Crawley, who ran the only motel in town, waved her hand at them, cutting Spring off. "Excuse me, but I asked for my eggs to be medium, not runny."

"I guess I better get back to work." Spring gave him a weak smile. "Besides, I promised that there would be no excuses if I messed up. So goodbye, Sheriff Kendall. I appreciate the opportunity to prove my worth."

When he couldn't think of anything to say to that, she turned away and took Mrs. Crawley's plate. "Sorry about that, Mrs. Crawley. I'll get Stella to make you some more." She took the plate to the order window and rang the bell. "Eggs are running and need to be caught!" Then she headed over to a booth full of cowboys, pulled out a pad, and started taking their order.

Waylon should just count his blessings and leave. His life would be much simpler if he didn't have to deal with Spring Hadley. But he didn't leave. Instead, he walked into the kitchen.

"Hey, Sheriff," Stella Sanders greeted him, "you want me to whip you up your usual scrambled eggs and bacon?"

"No, thank you. I already had some cereal this morning. Where's Carly?"

"She came down sick. She said it was the flu just like Bella has." She paused and leaned in closer. "But personally, I think that gal is in the family way. 'Course, I'm not one to poke my nose where it don't belong."

That would explain why Carly had been so tired

lately. It would also explain why Spring was there working. "Carly called Spring to help out?"

"No. That sweet little thang just showed up and volunteered. She's not very good at waitressing. Not one order she's taken has been right. But people don't seem to mind too much. It's hard to be mad at someone as friendly and sweet as Spring. The townsfolk were about ready to lynch me until she showed up and flashed that pretty little smile." Stella went back to flipping her pancakes. "You sure I can't make you something to eat? Cereal isn't enough to fill up a strapping man like you." She tossed him a wink. He had flirted a lot with Stella when he was deputy. As the sheriff, he needed to be more professional. So he ignored her flirting.

"No, thank you. I need to get back to the office." He walked out into the diner and watched Spring hustling around.

Stella was right. She wasn't a very good waitress. She splashed water on customers when she was filling their glasses, forgot to bring syrup with the pancakes, confused orders, and dropped Mrs. Crawley's plate of over medium eggs on the way to her table. But people didn't seem to mind her inefficiency—probably because it came with a cheerful smile and friendly chatter about everything from the weather to the upcoming spring dance.

She finally noticed Waylon standing there watching her. "Did I get your coffee wrong, Sheriff? I thought you liked it straight. No sugar or cream."

He took a sip and nodded. "It's perfect. I'll take it the exact same way tomorrow—that's if you don't mind making me a cup when you get to work."

She stared at him. "Work?"

"Sometimes there are good excuses for not showing up." He pulled on his hat. "I'll see you at seven thirty tomorrow morning, Miss Hadley."

Her blue eyes widened. "You're not firing me?"

"I can't fire a person I haven't even hired."

Her smile was as bright as the sun shining in through the windows. "I'll see you at seven thirty sharp tomorrow morning, Sheriff Kendall."

He paused. "Make that seven fifteen. There's a little business we need to discuss about touching my personal computer."

The smile slipped, and her cheeks turned pink. "I was just trying—"

He cut her off. "I don't care what you thought you were trying to do. My personal life is my personal life. Understood?"

She nodded before her eyes twinkled. "But I bet it worked. I bet you got some messages from ladies dying to go out with a man who knows how to smile, has no pet peeves, and loves romantic comedies and children's books."

He bit back a smile and tipped his hat. "Have a good day, Miss Hadley."

She sent him a sassy look. "You too, Alice."

Waylon spent the rest of the morning dealing with paperwork. At lunchtime he had a strong urge to go over to the diner. Instead, he finished up his reports, then went home and made himself a bologna sandwich with stale bread and iffy bologna. He took the sandwich and a glass of iced tea out to the porch where Sherlock was napping. The dog barely opened an eye when Waylon sat down in the rocker.

Waylon's house was one of the oldest houses in Bliss. It had been built in the early 1900s by a pretentious banker who wanted to impress the town. The Victorian-style house *was* impressive with its three-stories, wide wraparound porch, and ornate corbels. And Waylon's mother had been thrilled when her new husband bought it for her. Unfortunately, it had been nothing but a money pit to Waylon's father. From the wiring to the plumbing, something was always going wrong in the hundred-year-old house.

Still, Waylon loved it as much as his mother had. He loved the long wooden bannister that he and his brothers used to slide down, and the big kitchen where the entire family used to eat their meals. He loved the huge backyard where they'd had neighborhood barbecues and baseball games. He loved the attic that his mother had transformed into her reading room. Whenever he'd gotten tired of playing ball or roughhousing with his brothers, he'd gone up to the attic and laid down next to his mother on the old sofa that his grandmother had given her. His mother would read and run her fingers through his hair in a soothing way that always put him to sleep. And one of her favorite books to read to him had been *Alice in Wonderland*.

He missed his mom. He missed his entire family. The house was too big for one person. He pulled his phone from his pocket and tapped the online dating app. Thirty minutes later, he'd sent "hugs" to ten women.

After lunch, he checked in with Tucker, then

patrolled the town. He gave a citation to Jeff Winters for parking in a handicapped space and one to Tiffany Mueller for speeding—although the young teenager had done her best to talk him out of it by flirting and batting her eyelashes. On his way past the diner, he noticed that Spring's Jeep was no longer parked in front, so he stopped and checked in on Stella. The evening wait staff had shown up and things seemed to be running smoothly. Dinner and lunch were always slower than breakfast.

Once he finished his patrol, he swung by his house and changed into sweats and running shoes before he headed out to the Tender Heart Ranch. Raff, with the help of Luke and Savannah, had done a lot to the place in the last year. The barn had been painted a bright red and the old log cabin had new windows and a brand-new porch. Raff and Luke were standing in front of the porch throwing a baseball back and forth when Waylon pulled up.

"Hey, Way!" Raff said as soon as Waylon got out of his truck. "I'm glad you could stop by and give me your thoughts on the new addition."

"My pleasure." He lifted a hand to Luke. "Hey, Luke, how's it going?" Luke barely lifted a hand. Which made Waylon wonder how well this entire plan was going to work. It was obvious that the kid still held a grudge against Waylon for taking him into custody when he'd run away from home.

"I'll walk you around the back and show you where I want to add on in just a minute," Raff said. "Right now I need to call Savannah before she leaves Home Sweet Home and ask her to stop by the grocery store and grab some milk." He shot a glance at Luke. "This one goes through milk like a starving calf." He held out his glove and ball to Waylon. "Why don't you and Luke toss the ball while I'm inside? Luke is on the baseball team this season."

Waylon tried to look surprised. "Really?" He took the glove and ball. "What position?"

When Luke didn't answer, Raff answered for him. "He wants to pitch." He sent Waylon a can-you-friggin'-believe-it look before he headed toward the cabin. "I'll be right back."

Once Raff was gone, Waylon tugged on the glove. "So have you pitched before? Maybe in Little League?"

"I didn't do Little League." Luke glared at him. "And I know what you and Raff are up to. Raff has been telling me what a great baseball player you were in high school and college for the last week. Then suddenly you show up in your sweats and want to toss around the ball. You're here to coach me at baseball, aren't you? You're here because Raff thinks I suck."

Waylon hadn't minded keeping his mouth shut about Raff's plan, but he couldn't out-and-out lie to Luke. "Raff just wants you to succeed. He knows how much it means to you, and he thought I could give you a few pointers."

"What makes you so great? If you were any good, you would be playing in the pros."

"I wanted to play in the pros. I got drafted by the Dodgers my senior year of high school, but my parents talked me into going to college first. My junior year of college, I tore my Achilles tendon and didn't even make the draft."

Luke looked surprised. "You got drafted right

out of high school? What round?"

"The ninth."

"Damn." Luke punched his fist in his glove. "You should've gone."

Waylon had struggled with the same regret for years. He loved baseball and wished he'd gotten a chance to play in the big leagues. "Yeah. I should've. But sometimes life leads you in a different direction than you intended." He threw the ball straight to Luke. It hit his glove but bounced back out before he could catch it. It looked like Raff was right. Luke's baseball skills did need some work.

Luke leaned down and picked up the ball. "So you didn't want to be a sheriff?" He threw the ball to Waylon.

Waylon had to stretch to catch it. "I didn't say that. I've always wanted to follow in my father's footsteps. But who wouldn't want to play in the pros if they got a chance?" He tossed the ball back and forth with Luke a few times before he asked, "Did your coach ever teach you about the four-seam grip?"

"What's that?"

Obviously, Luke's coach hadn't taught him the basics. Probably because most high school kids already knew them. If they hadn't learned from their dads, they learned from their coaches in Little League. Luke hadn't had either. That made Waylon even more determined to help him.

"It's the best way to hold a ball if you want a powerful, straight throw." He held up the ball and demonstrated. "You place the middle and index fingers of your throwing hand perpendicular to the horseshoe of the seam. That way your fingers will be in the perfect position to use the seams of the ball to pull down as you throw and get maximum backward rotation. When the ball spins like that it flies true and straight. Squat down and hold your glove up." He threw the ball hard, and it hit the center of Luke's glove with a loud smack of leather.

The kid grinned from ear to ear. "Sweet."

"Now you try."

The throw was better but was still weak and inaccurate. Waylon walked over and showed Luke again. This time, he adjusted Luke's hands on the ball before he walked back to his spot. He barely had time to turn around before the ball came whizzing toward him. He caught it before it hit him right between the eyes.

He lowered the glove. "Sweet. But next time wait until I'm ready."

They continued to throw the ball back and forth. With each throw, Luke grew more confident and accurate. The February evening air held just enough chill, and the sound of smacking leather was soothing and familiar. When he was a kid, Waylon and his brothers had played catch with their dad every night in the backyard until his mother had yelled for them to wash up for dinner. He'd loved those evenings playing catch. He'd forgotten how much until now.

After being injured and passed up by the draft, he'd been angry and resentful. He'd given away his favorite baseball glove and refused any offers to play on recreational leagues. He didn't even like to watch it on television. Now he realized how childish he'd been. Just because he couldn't play as a professional didn't mean he couldn't still enjoy the sport. He was enjoying it with Luke now. In fact, he felt the tension he'd been carrying in his neck and shoulders loosening and relaxing.

"So be honest," he said as he threw the ball to Luke. "Why do you suddenly want to play baseball when you've never played the sport before?"

Luke caught the ball and glanced at the cabin. "Because I really suck at football."

"Excuse me?"

Luke stared down at the ball in his glove. "Raff played football in high school. His name is even up on the gym wall. I know I can never get my name on a wall, but I was hoping I could play something that would make him . . ." He let the sentence drift off, but Waylon got it. Luke wanted to make Raff proud.

Damned if that didn't make Waylon almost tear up. The kid had been through hell with his abusive stepfather and according to Raff, his biological father hadn't been much better. He had run off when Luke was a baby and never come back. Raff was the first man who had ever shown Luke any kind of love and affection, and Luke felt like he had to prove he was worthy of that love.

Waylon wanted to tell him that Raff would love him whether he played baseball or not. But he knew that a few kind words wouldn't get rid of Luke's insecurities. He had to get over those on his own. And maybe baseball would help him do that.

"Okay," Waylon held out his glove. "Throw me the heater."

The ball Luke threw was far from a ninety-mile-an-hour heater, but everyone had to start somewhere.

CHAPTER ELEVEN

WORKING FOR WAYLON WASN'T EASY. The man was a perfectionist and had high expectations of his assistant. According to him, Spring wasn't even close to being as proficient as saintly Gail. She couldn't do reports as well. She couldn't take messages as well. She couldn't keep her desk as neat and clean.

The first two weeks, she seemed to get everything wrong. Except the coffee. To save herself time, she had stopped picking it up at the diner and had started making it at the office. It was the only thing he didn't complain about. Of course, he didn't thank her for it either. Or for ordering him lunch every day from the diner. And dinner if he was working late.

His lack of appreciation had started to tick her off, and there had been more than a few times when she'd wanted to throw in the towel and quit. The only thing that kept her from it was her desire to prove to her family that she wasn't an irresponsible ditz. No matter what it took, she was going to keep her job, pay for the repairs to her Jeep, and go

on a camping adventure. Although it didn't look
like her daddy would be joining her. She'd left him
three messages detailing her plan and how much
fun they would have, and he'd yet to answer her.
Which made her start to wonder if he'd changed
at all, and if she was just a gullible fool to believe
that he had.

"Miss Hadley!"

Spring quickly slipped on her high heels and got
up from her desk. Before she stepped into Waylon's
office, she smoothed out the skirt of her bright
green dress and pinned on a big smile. The smile
faded when she saw Waylon.

Earlier that morning, he had looked as spit-and-
polished as he always did. Every golden-brown hair
had been in place, and his shirt was stiffly starched
and buttoned at the cuffs. But this afternoon, his
hair looked like he'd been running his fingers
through it, his shirt was limp and wrinkled, and
his cuffs were unbuttoned and folded back. Since
it was the first time she'd seen his forearms, she
couldn't keep her gaze off the muscles that flexed
when he turned his computer monitor to her.

"What's this?"

She looked at the monitor and bit back a smile.
"It's three cute little pugs in pink tutus."

He took a deep breath and slowly released it.
"What are those pugs doing on my screensaver?"

It had been an impulsive decision. She'd been
placing copies of the reports she'd finished on his
desk when his screensaver had popped up. The
Texas flag with the words *Protect and Serve* written
across the image in big, bold letters was honor-
able. It was also the last thing Waylon needed to

be reminded of every time he sat down at his computer. The man put enough pressure on himself to protect and serve. He certainly didn't need any more. So she'd changed it to something a little more lighthearted.

She looked at the pugs. "They appear to be dancing."

She expected him to let her have it like he had when she'd called Miley Gaines's ex-boyfriend and asked him to return her Garth Brooks CDs because he might be hurt over the break up, but he couldn't ask her to return a gift. Or when she told Glen Stafford that having a neighbor who grew marijuana might not be such a bad thing. Or when she gave Jonas a neck pillow to use when he took naps while on patrol.

But Waylon didn't get mad at her. Instead, he leaned back in his chair, closed his eyes, and didn't say another word. She stared at him in confusion and finally noticed his flushed face.

"Are you okay?"

He kept his eyes closed. "I'm fine. I just have a headache. Do you have any aspirin?"

"No, but I think I might have some Advil." She went back to her desk and searched through her purse. She had just pulled out the small bottle when the phone rang. It was Mrs. Miller. The woman called daily with one complaint or another. Spring knew she was lonely after her grandchildren had moved and always spent a good fifteen minutes chatting with her. But last night she'd had an epiphany and thought she'd figured out a long-term solution to Mrs. Miller's loneliness.

"Hi, Mrs. Miller. I'm so glad you called. I have

something I wanted to talk to you about."

"Has the sheriff done something about all the unneutered cats running around?"

"Actually, he has been pretty busy. But I talked with Joanna Daily and she's going to see if the vet will be willing to offer discounted spaying and neutering to pet owners."

"That's wonderful! I don't think I can fit one more stray cat or kitten in my house. I can't thank you enough, Spring. You're the only one who really seems to care, and if there's anything I can do for you, you just let me know."

"Actually, there is. My sister-in-law Gracie has been looking for someone to help her with the triplets. And since you took care of your grandchildren before they moved, I thought you might be interested." There was a long stretch of silence, and Spring wondered if she'd made a mistake. "I realize three babies is a lot so if you don't—"

Mrs. Miller cut her off. "I'd love to watch those sweet little girls. I would've said something to Gracie myself, but I thought she was looking for a young girl to help her, not an old grandma."

"I think a granny nanny is exactly what she's looking for." Thirty minutes later, Spring had talked to Gracie and had everything arranged between her and Mrs. Miller. Both seemed thrilled with the solution, and Spring couldn't help feeling pretty pleased with herself for thinking of it. At least she was pleased with herself until she noticed the bottle of Advil sitting on the desk. Shoot! She'd forgotten all about Waylon.

She grabbed the bottle, filled a glass of water from the water fountain, and hurried into Waylon's office. "I'm sorry. Mrs. Miller called and—" She cut off when she saw Waylon huddled beneath his heavy sheriff's jacket, shivering as if he were freezing.

"Oh my gosh, you're sick." She moved around desk and set down the bottle of ibuprofen and the water and placed a hand on his forehead. His skin was burning up with fever.

He pulled away. "I'm not s-s-sick." His teeth chattered. "There must be something wrong with the thermostat. First it was too hot, and now it's too cold."

"That's because you have a raging fever." She stared at him, unsure of what to do. She had never been very good with sick people—that was Autumn's thing. But since Autumn wasn't there, it was up to her. "We need to get you to the doctor."

"I'm not going to the doctor. It's probably just the flu. It's going around." Waylon pushed down his jacket and reached for the bottle of Advil, but his hands shook so badly he couldn't open the lid.

She took it from him and opened it. "Then you need to go home and go to bed." She tapped out three tablets and waited for him to toss them into his mouth before she handed him the water.

He downed the entire glass. "I can't go home. I have a meeting with the other county sheriffs at two o'clock."

"You'll have to cancel. You can't go to a meeting when you're sick."

"I can't cancel. I'll be fine in a few minutes." A chill racked his body and all the color left his face.

The man was so stubborn. But Spring was stubborn too. She didn't say another word as she walked out and closed the door behind her. The first person she called was the sheriff in charge of the meeting. She explained the situation, and the sheriff was more than sympathetic.

"Those spring colds are hell," he said. "You tell Waylon to take care of himself and I'll have my assistant send him the minutes of the meeting. If he has any questions, he can call me."

Once she finished talking with the sheriff, she called Tucker to see if he could come take care of the office, then she called the only person she could think of to get Waylon to listen to reason. A few minutes after she'd hung up the phone, the door to Waylon's office flew open, and he appeared in the doorway looking haggard—and pissed.

"You called my mother?"

She smiled sweetly as she got up and hooked her purse over her shoulder. "Drastic times call for drastic measures. And if you don't want me to call her back, you'd better let me take you home."

He pouted the entire drive home. Pouted and shivered with fever.

She had never been to his house and was surprised when he grouchily pointed it out. She had expected him to live in a sterile home with an immaculate lawn and nothing out of place. But the three-story Victorian wasn't sterile. It was grand yet homey with a big yard filled with flower beds, dog toys, and cute little garden gnomes.

"You live here?" He didn't answer, and when she glanced over, she saw that he was shivering even harder. "Come on, let's get you into bed."

The inside of the house looked as lived-in as the outside. Hooks with a profusion of coats and cowboy hats hung just inside the door, a couple pairs of muddy cowboy boots beneath. A snap-down western shirt hung over the bannister and more dog toys lay in the middle of the dark wood floor of the foyer.

His upstairs bedroom was messier than downstairs. Jeans and boxer briefs littered the floor and the huge king-sized bed was unmade. Obviously, he was only fussy about his job, and she had to wonder how hard it was for him to be so meticulous at work when it obviously wasn't his nature.

"Do you need me to help you get into your pajamas?" she asked, when he sat down on the bed and tugged off his boots.

"No. You can leave now."

She probably should've left. But instead she went down to the kitchen and made him some tea. While she was heating the water, Joanna Daily came in the back door with Sherlock. Ms. Marble followed behind. Joanna looked surprised to see Spring; Ms. Marble not at all. In fact, her aging blue eyes twinkled.

Just so the woman didn't get the wrong idea, Spring quickly explained. "Waylon came down with the flu. I'm just making him some hot tea before I leave."

"Oh no," Joanna said as she took off Sherlock's leash. "I hope it's not the same virus that Emmett caught. It only lasts twenty-four hours, but he was miserable for every second of that time."

Spring scratched Sherlock's ears. "Waylon is pretty miserable. I'm wondering if I should take him to the doctor."

"I took Emmett, and it was a waste of time. There

was nothing the doctor could do. If it's the same virus, it just has to run its course."

"That's nice to hear. I was worried about leaving Waylon by himself."

"'Oh, you can't leave Waylon by himself, Spring,'" Ms. Marble said. "You'll need to stay right here and keep an eye on him."

"I don't think she needs—" Joanna started, but Ms. Marble cut her off.

"Now, Jo, you said yourself how miserable Emmett was and how much care he needed. We can't leave our sheriff to take care of himself. Not when he works so hard to take care of this entire town." Ms. Marble sent Joanna a pointed look from beneath her wide sun hat. Having grown up with sisters, Spring knew that look. It was a don't-argue-just-go-along-with-me look. Joanna read it immediately.

"You're right, Maybelline. We certainly couldn't do that." She looked at Spring. "I would volunteer to look after the sheriff, but I'm afraid I'm swamped with everything that still needs to be done for the spring dance."

"And I have five dozen cupcakes to make for Noel Thurman's son's birthday party tomorrow," Ms. Marble said. "But I'll be happy to stop by in the morning and relieve you, Spring."

Spring's eyes widened. "Relieve me? I'm not staying the night here."

Ms. Marble's face got the stern teacher look she used whenever she wanted someone to do something. The look could make you crumble in a hurry. "I'm afraid you have to. You're Waylon's assistant. And he needs assistance right now."

"But—"

"No buts. I'll bring some of my cinnamon swirl muffins in the morning."

Joanna moved to the door. "And I'll run over to the house and get some NyQuil. It was the only thing that helped Emmett sleep and brought down his fever."

"Good idea, Jo," Ms. Marble said. "Men are much better patients when they're drugged." She patted Spring's shoulder. "Don't look so nervous, dear. All you have to do is keep an eye on him. Waylon has always been a man who can be trusted to behave like a gentleman."

Spring knew the two were matchmaking, but they were also right. She couldn't leave Waylon alone. If she did, she'd be worried about him all night.

After Joanna and Ms. Marble left, she finished making Waylon's tea. Before she could take it up to him, Joanna came back with the medicine.

"Just use the little cup on the lid to measure out the correct dosage. We don't want to overdose our sheriff."

Spring thanked her, and once she was gone, took the medicine and tea upstairs. When she got to Waylon's room, he was sound asleep. So she left the tea and medicine on his nightstand and quietly closed the door.

She used the new cellphone she'd bought with her first paycheck to call Tucker and make sure everything was okay at the office. When she informed him that neither she nor the sheriff would be in to work in the morning, Tucker reacted like an overeager puppy.

"You tell the sheriff not to worry about a thing. Tucker Riddell has got everything under control."

After calling Tucker, she called Gracie and let her know that she couldn't make it to dinner because she was working late. It wasn't exactly a lie. Like Ms. Marble said, she *was* assisting the sheriff. She just didn't think that her brother would be happy about her assisting Waylon in his house overnight. She wasn't exactly happy about it either.

At least, she wasn't to begin with. But then she discovered the room in the attic with the over-stuffed couch and the shelves and shelves of books. Spring loved to read and hadn't had much time since starting Seasons with her sisters. She scanned the titles on the shelves, and when she found *Alice in Wonderland*, she pulled it out and settled down on the couch to read. She got so lost in the story that she paid no attention to the time until the room filled with the first purple of twilight.

She put down the book and went down the stairs to check on Waylon. He was still sleeping. Although it looked like he had been awake. The tea was gone . . . and so was the bottle of NyQuil. She was sure it had been half full when Joanna had brought it over. She remembered Joanna's parting words and couldn't help freaking out. It would not look good on her resume if the sheriff died from a drug overdose on her watch.

She hurried to the bed. "Sheriff Kendall?" When he didn't move, she reached out and touched his shoulder. It was cool to the touch. Which worried her even more. Didn't people lose all body heat when they died? She tried to shake him, but it was like trying to shake an oak tree. Her voice got louder and more panicked. "Waylon, wake up. Come on now. Just for a second. Just until I make sure that you're in the land of the living."

When he didn't respond, she sat down on the bed and pulled back the sheet from his shoulders. She might've stopped to admire the smooth muscled beauty of his naked chest if she hadn't been so concerned. When she saw the slight rise and fall of his breathing, she said a prayer of thanks that he wasn't dead. Still, she wouldn't be happy until he opened his eyes and spoke to her.

"Waylon." She leaned over him and gently tapped his stubbled jaw "Wake up. Please wake up." He didn't open his eyes, and her tapping became a little more frantic until she finally just hauled off and slapped him. The sound of her palm hitting his cheek resounded in the twilight-lit room like a firecracker. His eyes finally slid open.

They stared back at her, unfocused and feverish. "Spring?"

She sagged with relief, resting her forehead on his chest. "You scared me."

He spoke in a husky voice that vibrated through her. "You scare me." Before she could figure out what he meant, his fingers slid through her hair and lifted her head. She got a glimpse of molten green eyes before he covered her mouth with his lips.

She was stunned. Not just that he'd kissed her, but by the way he kissed her. He didn't kiss like she'd thought a strait-laced sheriff would kiss. He followed no rules as his lips hungrily slid over hers. The inside of his mouth was hot and wet and his tongue teasing and seductive as he took a deep, thorough taste. When she finally found the strength to pull away, she was feeling like she'd drunk half a bottle of cold medicine.

"You kissed me." It was the dumbest thing she'd ever said in her life. But before her cheeks could fill with heat, Waylon's eyes closed. A few seconds later, he started to snore. Not a little snore, but a big, rumbling snore like a bear in hibernation.

She sat back and tried to catch her breath and reason with herself. The kiss meant nothing. Waylon hadn't been in his right mind. He probably wouldn't even remember it in the morning.

But Spring would.

Spring would remember that kiss for the rest of her life.

CHAPTER TWELVE

THE RINGING OF HIS PHONE pulled Waylon out of a deep sleep. He groggily reached for the nightstand, but his phone wasn't there. By the time he opened his eyes to the pinkish rays of dawn, the ringing had stopped. It started back up again only seconds later. He sat up and glanced around. The ring was coming from his shirt on the floor. He got up and took the phone from the pocket, then glanced at the caller ID before he answered.

"Good morning, Mom."

"It's good to know that my oldest son is alive and well."

He stretched the muscles in his shoulders. "A little achy, but much better than I was yesterday."

"That's what a little bed rest will do for you. You should be thankful your assistant called me when she did."

He scowled as he walked into the bathroom. Spring had no business calling his mother—something he intended to get straight with her as soon as he got into the office this morning.

"She sounded like such a sweet girl on the phone," his mom continued. "And I'm thrilled you have someone to help you while Gail's gone." She paused. "Especially a pretty, young, single woman."

He knew where this was going. "No, Mother."

"No, what?"

"No, I'm not going to date my assistant. Not only is Spring not my type, interoffice dating is against office policy." He turned on the shower and caught a glimpse of himself in the mirror over the sink. He looked like crap. His eyes were red-rimmed and his face a sickly pale . . . except for the red marks on the left side of his jaw. He squinted and leaned closer to the mirror. The pillow creases almost looked like a handprint.

"Well, all I can say is it's a relief to know someone is looking after you."

He rubbed the pillow creases. "I'm a big boy, Mom. I don't need looking after."

"Everyone needs someone to look out for them. And since your father and I aren't there, I worry. It would be so nice if you could find someone special like your brothers did. What about online dating? Melanie Hartman's son found the love of his life that way."

Waylon hadn't told his mom about joining the online dating site. He didn't want her calling him every day asking if he'd found a wife. He wasn't looking for a wife. He was just looking for woman who looked at him as a man, instead of as Sheriff Kendall. And surprisingly, he might've found one.

Lynn was one of the first women to send him a "hug." They had been messaging back and forth for the last week and seemed to have a lot of things in common. She was a business owner who was as devoted to her job as he was. She came from a close-knit family that could sometimes be a little too close-knit. She was addicted to coffee and loved dogs—her profile picture was of a cute black Labrador. And best of all, she lived completely out of his jurisdiction. They hadn't set a date to meet yet, but Waylon planned to ask her soon.

"Stop worrying about my love life, Mom," he said. "I'm fine."

"You'd be even finer if you found someone to care for."

"I have someone to care for. In fact, I have an entire town of someones to care for. Speaking of which, I need to take a shower and get to work. I'll call you later."

He hung up and got in the shower. The heat helped ease his aching muscles, and by the time he got out, he felt more like himself. He walked out of the bathroom and noticed that Sherlock wasn't in his dog bed. Which meant that Joanna Daily had come early to walk him. He felt bad about leaving his neighbor to always walk his dog, so he got dressed quickly, thinking he'd catch up to her and take over.

But as he was pulling on his boots, he heard singing. And it wasn't Joanna Daily's voice. It was the same voice that came from his receptionist's area every day. Spring was one of those people who burst out in song for no reason whatsoever. Obviously, she'd come over this morning to check on him. He could only hope that she'd brought coffee. His head still felt a little fuzzy, and he could use some caffeine to get focused.

When he stepped out of his room, he realized that the singing wasn't coming from downstairs. It was coming from down the hallway. Confused, he followed the sound to the guest bathroom. What the hell was Spring doing in his bathroom? He knocked on the door repeatedly, and when she didn't answer, he turned the knob and peeked in.

She was sitting in the claw foot tub with her back to him and one leg pointed up at the ceiling as she lathered it with soap. A pair of hot pink ear buds sprouted from her ears, the cord trailing to her phone, which sat on the floor next to the dog. Sherlock opened one bloodshot eye and looked at Waylon before he closed it and went back to sleep. Waylon let his gaze wander over that long, water-slick leg and her pale soft-looking shoulders before he closed the door.

He stood there for a moment and allowed his breathing to return to normal, then he turned and headed to the spare bedroom. The bed covers were mussed, and the clothes Spring had worn the day before were scattered on the floor. He leaned down and picked up a pair of pink panties that were not much bigger than a postage stamp. He was rubbing the satiny material between his fingers when Ms. Marble's voice caused him to freeze.

"Good morning."

Waylon dropped the panties and turned to find the older woman standing in the doorway. She wasn't wearing her usual big sunbonnet, but she was wearing a knowing smile.

"I knocked on the back door," she said, "but I guess you couldn't hear me with all the singing going on." She glanced down at Spring's panties. "I see you had an overnight guest."

"No!" He spoke the word much louder than he intended. Ms. Marble's eyebrows shot up, and he quickly amended the lie. "I mean, it's not how it looks. I was sick, and I didn't even know she had stayed the night until this morning when I walked in on her—" He cut off and his face heated.

Ms. Marble studied him like she'd done when he was in first grade and trying to get away with something. "Come down into the kitchen, Waylon, and I'll make you some coffee. You look like you could use some." She turned and headed down the stairs. Waylon followed like a naughty schoolboy who had just been caught tugging a little girl's braids.

In the kitchen, he started to help make the coffee, but Ms. Marble shook her head and pointed to a chair. "I'll get it. If I remember correctly, you make the worst coffee on both sides of the Pecos."

Once they were seated at the big oak table with their cups of coffee and a plate of cinnamon swirl muffins, Ms. Marble pinned him with her intense eyes. "I know why Spring is here, Waylon. Jo and I didn't think you should be alone when you were so sick. And since we were both busy, we asked Spring to stay and keep an eye on you. I'm surprised she didn't explain everything last night."

"I was a little out of it last night." He suddenly remembered waking up with a splitting headache and drinking the NyQuil. He had just assumed that Spring had put it there before she left. But she hadn't left. She'd slept in his guest room and taken a bath in his tub . . . naked. He pushed the thought of soft shoulders and one mile-long sudsy leg out of his mind and cleared his throat.

"You shouldn't have asked her to stay," he said. "It's not proper."

Ms. Marble stared at him. "Proper?"

"It doesn't look good. Which is why it would be best if you and Joanna didn't tell anyone Spring stayed the night. I wouldn't want people to get the wrong idea."

Ms. Marble set down her cup. "Maybe it's time people got the wrong idea, Waylon."

"Excuse me?"

Her steel blue eyes pierced right through him. "The transition from deputy to sheriff has been a tough one for you, hasn't it?"

He wanted to deny it and act like it was no big deal, but he had never been able to lie to Ms. Marble. "My father left big shoes to fill."

"Then why try to fill them?" She reached out and patted his hand. "Your father was a wonderful sheriff, and this town loved him. We still do. But your father isn't our sheriff anymore, Waylon. You are. And we didn't vote you in to fill your father's shoes. We voted you in to fill your own. You need to figure out how you want to sheriff this town. You don't need to figure out how your father did."

He was so taken aback it took him a while to reply. "But being tough and respected was how he kept this town safe."

"I'm not telling you that there won't be times that you need to be tough. But there are also times you need to—how do young people say it—lighten up. Not only with the people of this town, but also with yourself. It's no one's business who stays the night with you. Or why they stay the night. Unless you're doing something illegal, you have a right to your own private life. You have a right to have a beer at the Watering Hole." Her eyes twinkled. "Or have a young woman spend the night. Bliss isn't just the place you work. It's your home."

Before he could reply, she got to her feet. "Now I need to be going. Carly is still struggling with her morning sickness so I promised her I'd help out in the mornings at the diner." As she was putting on her hat, Sherlock came into the room. She gave the dog a pat on the head before she walked out the door.

When Ms. Marble was gone, Waylon just sat there trying to process what she'd said. Was she right? Was he so busy trying to fill his father's shoes that he'd lost himself? The feel of Sherlock's wet nose on his hand pulled him out of his musings. He scratched the dog's ears then got up to get him breakfast. He was bent over pouring dog food in Sherlock's bowl when he noticed Spring standing in the doorway. She was dressed in the same clothes she'd worn the day before. Her short hair was damp and her face flushed. The image of her in the bathtub popped into his mind, and his face filled with heat . . . along with the rest of his body.

He looked away and finished filling Sherlock's bowl. "Good morning." When she didn't reply, he glanced back to find her still standing there, fidgeting with the wrinkled skirt of her dress. Since Spring had never acted hesitant and shy before, he was immediately wary.

"Are you okay?" he asked.

Her gaze settled on his mouth, then quickly skittered away. "I'm fine. Just fine. How are you feeling?"

"Much better." He paused. "Thank you for staying and keeping an eye on me."

The color in her cheeks deepened. "You're welcome."

They should both get going—Waylon to the office and Spring to change her clothes. But after Ms. Marble's lecture, he decided a few more minutes wouldn't hurt anything. He owned Spring more than just a thank you. He pulled out a chair at the table. "Sit down and I'll get you a cup of coffee. I don't have that fancy creamer you like, but I've got milk and plenty of sugar."

She hesitated as if she were afraid to move closer to him. And he figured she had a right to be. He'd been a snarling bear yesterday. "Look, I'm sorry about being so grumpy yesterday. I guess I'm not a good patient."

Her gaze returned to his mouth. "You weren't that bad." She shook her head as if to clear it and glanced at the table. "I see Ms. Marble brought muffins."

He wiped at his mouth, wondering if he had toothpaste on the corners. "Along with plenty of advice." He walked to the cupboard and got down a cup. "She thinks I need to . . . lighten up."

Spring laughed. "Leave it to Ms. Marble to hit the nail on the head."

He frowned as he poured coffee in the cup. "I'm the sheriff. Sheriffs aren't supposed to be cuddly teddy bears."

"No, but a few smiles wouldn't hurt anything. Nor would a few days off. When was the last time you took a full day off?"

"I have Sundays off." He added sugar, then walked to the refrigerator for the milk.

"Don't act like you have Sundays off. Jonas told me you still stop by the office and take calls. That's not a day off. I'm talking about letting Tucker and Jonas handle things for an entire day while you do whatever it is you like to do."

He poured some milk into the coffee and then carried the cup to the table. "Tucker is still too new and I should probably fire Jonas. But he'd be lost without his job."

"The poor man is still grieving for his wife. When he stops by to check on me at night, she's all he can talk about." She took the cup of coffee.

He sat down. "He comes out to check on you?"

"Like Mrs. Miller, I think he just wants to talk. And I don't mind the company." She took a sip of coffee. "This is a nice change. I'm usually making you coffee."

"Ms. Mable made this." He took a sip. "Coffee making isn't my strong suit."

"But you're good at more important things." She took a muffin off the plate. "I'm good at unimportant things—like making coffee."

"Believe me, coffee's important. And you're good at other things. You've been a big help to me the last couple weeks."

She glanced up from peeling the wrapper off the muffin. Her big blue eyes held surprise. "Is that a compliment? Or are you still high on NyQuil?" Her gaze traveled down to his mouth, and her cheeks blushed a bright pink.

He set down his cup. "What's going on?"

Her eyes flashed up. "W-w-what do you mean?"

"You aren't a blusher, and yet, all you've done this morning is blush." He paused as a thought struck him. "Did something happen last night? Did I . . ." He rubbed his jaw where the pillow creases had been. Pillow creases that looked suspiciously like fingerprints. "Did I try something?"

Spring's blush grew even darker, and she looked away. "It was nothing really. You drank too much cold medicine and got a little loopy." She set the muffin back down on the plate without taking a bite. "I better go. I need to change clothes and I don't want to be late for work." She started to get up, but he caught her wrist and stopped her.

"What happened? Did I do something I need to apologize for? Is that why you slapped me?"

She stared at his hand and refused to meet his gaze. "No. I was worried because you weren't responding to me so I slapped you to try and wake you up."

"Then why all the blushes?"

She visibly swallowed. "Because after I woke you up, you sorta . . . kissed me. But it really wasn't a big deal. It was just a kiss." She got up so quickly she tipped over her chair. Waylon caught it before it hit the floor. She grabbed her purse from the hook by the door and pulled her keys out of the side pocket. "I'll see you at the office." She dropped the keys, then quickly picked them up and dashed out the door as if her tail was on fire.

Waylon sat back in his chair. He'd kissed Spring? He shouldn't be surprised. She had the kind of lips that begged a man to kiss them. Being drugged and out of his head with fever, it made sense that he would try to take a taste. But it wasn't the kiss that bothered him as much as her reaction to it. Spring might say it wasn't a big deal, but if that were the case, then why was she so flustered? There seemed to be only one answer.

She'd liked his kiss.

Which wasn't a good thing. Having an assistant who had a crush on you would make for uncomfortable working conditions.

And yet, Waylon couldn't stop the satisfied smile that spread across his face.

CHAPTER THIRTEEN

S PRING WAS GOING TO HAVE to quit her job. She couldn't concentrate on work when all she could think about was Waylon's kiss. She couldn't be in the same room with the man without staring at his mouth. And the worst part about it was he knew how much she'd enjoyed his kiss. There was a gleam of male arrogance in his eyes every time he caught her staring, and he hadn't gotten after her once for being distracted and messing up phone messages or reports. She should've never told him about the kiss. Obviously, he'd been completely out of it and didn't remember it. But even if she hadn't told him, she'd still have the same problem.

She wanted a repeat. She wanted it in a bad way. She wanted Waylon to slide his fingers through her hair, to use his thumbs to tip up her chin, to cover her mouth with his wet heat and take a deep, satisfying sip that left her—

"Miss Hadley?"

She glanced up to see Waylon standing in front of her desk. Besides a few sniffles, he had recovered from his illness and was back to being the perfect sheriff. His hair was combed, his strong jaw clean-shaven, and his shirt starched. Although he had taken to rolling back the cuffs of the shirt and showing off his great forearm muscles and the black watch on one wrist. Who knew a timepiece could look so sexy?

He cleared his throat, and she pulled her gaze away from his watch to his twinkling green eyes. "I've been repeatedly calling your name, Miss Hadley. Do you have a hearing problem?"

She had a lust problem, but she couldn't exactly say that. "No, sir. I guess I was just daydreaming."

A wink of a smile flashed before it disappeared. "About anything in particular?"

She tried to come up with something that might take the annoying twinkle from his eyes. "I was just thinking about the spring dance. Tucker wants me to make sure I save him a dance."

The twinkle left his eyes, and one eyebrow lifted.

"What's the matter?" she asked. "Don't you like to dance?"

"I like to dance just fine."

"So you're going to the dance?"

"I always go. I have to keep an eye on things." He squinted. "Tucker? Isn't he a little young for you?"

Tucker was too young for her. He was like an overeager Labrador puppy she was trying to hold back so he wouldn't lick her in the face. Waylon, on the other hand, could lick her anywhere he wanted. She shook her head to get rid of the image and started organizing her messy desk.

"I'm not that old."

"Tucker is twenty-three."

"And I'm only twenty-eight. That's not that big

of an age difference. The age difference between us is larger." She could've kicked herself. Now he knew she'd been thinking about their age difference.

His forehead wrinkled, and he opened his mouth to say something, but then closed it again. He pulled on his cowboy hat. "I'm going to be out of the office for a couple hours. I should be back around five." He turned and walked out.

Once he was gone, Spring wilted back in her chair. She really needed to get a grip and quit acting like an idiot. So Waylon had kissed her. So what? She had been kissed by lots of boys. High school boys. College boys. Band boys. And maybe that was the difference. Waylon didn't kiss like a boy. He kissed like a man. A man who knew exactly what he wanted.

He'd wanted her.

A light bulb turned on in her head. She had been so worried about hiding her reaction to the kiss that she hadn't given much thought to why Waylon had kissed her in the first place. He'd been drugged and feverish, but not so drugged and feverish that he didn't know who she was. He'd said her name. He'd also said that she scared him. Why would she scare him . . . unless he was struggling with his sexual attraction to her as much as she was struggling with hers to him?

The thought made her feel less like an idiot. It also made her wonder how long they could avoid boinking on Waylon's desk. Just the thought of him bending her over his desk made her heart accelerate and her body flood with heat. She could only hope that Gail came back soon. Having sex with her boss would be an even bigger mistake than for-getting to lock up Seasons.

The phone rang, and she spent the next hour chatting with Mrs. Miller about how well her first day as a nanny for the triplets had gone. Halfway through the conversation, her head started to ache. By the time she hung up, she had a splitting head-ache. She took a couple of ibuprofen, but they didn't seem to help. When the chills started, she realized she'd gotten more from Waylon's kiss than a bad case of desire.

"Are you okay?" Jonas asked when he arrived for his evening shift. He placed a big box on the floor by her desk. "You don't look so good."

She shivered and pulled the keys from the top drawer. "I think I'm coming down with the flu. Do you think you could keep an eye on things until Waylon gets back?"

"Sure. But maybe I better drive you home?"

"No, thank you. I'll be fine once I get some rest." She got up. "What's in the box?"

Jonas's eyes turned sad. "Some of Meg's sweat-ers and costume jewelry that I thought you might like." He paused. "I've decided it's time to clean out her closet, and I know she would've loved a pretty young woman like you getting use out of her things."

It was a big step for him, and Spring knew it. If she hadn't been sick, she would've given him a big hug. "Thank you, Jonas. I'll treasure them."

He nodded and picked up the box. "I'll put it in your car."

Her chills were even worse by the time she got back to her trailer. All she wanted to do was wrap up in her fluffy down comforter and sleep. But when she stepped into her trailer, there was already someone sprawled out in her small bed.

"Hey, Spring-a-ling." Her father flashed a smile, then toasted her with the can of beer in his hand. "You surprised to see your old man?"

She was surprised. And a little annoyed. She'd called him numerous times, and he hadn't called her back once. Then he just shows up at her trailer without a word? She set the box Jonas had given her on the floor by the door, then put her purse and keys on the kitchenette counter. "How did you get in? And where's your car?"

"You know that I've always had a way with locks. And I parked around back." He took a deep drag of the cigarette in his other hand and blew smoke directly at her. She coughed and fanned the smoke away. She should've said something about him smoking in her trailer, but she didn't. Mainly because she didn't have the strength. She barely had the strength to flop down on the bench seat of the table.

"You should've called first," she said as she rubbed her aching temples. "It won't be pretty when Dirk finds out you're here."

"I guess that boy is still holding a grudge against his dear old daddy."

She lifted her head and stared at him. "You tried to take Gracie and Cole's ranch, Daddy. Anyone would hold a grudge about that."

"Those Arringtons have plenty of money to spare. One little ol' ranch wasn't going to make a difference one way or the other. Besides, I didn't come to see Dirk. I came to go camping with my favorite girl."

She should have been thrilled. It was what she wanted. She wanted to prove to her family that he'd changed. But as she studied her father through the haze of cigarette smoke, her vision cleared. Maybe it was the fever, or maybe Granny Bon was right. Maybe Spring needed time away from her sisters to grow up and stop viewing the world through rose-colored glasses. Whatever it was, she suddenly realized that Holt hadn't changed at all.

He had no regret over trying to take Cole's ranch. He didn't think there was anything wrong with breaking into a person's home. And he thought it was just fine and dandy to not answer her calls, and then show up out of the blue. It was exactly what he had done all Spring's life. She and her family wouldn't hear a word from him for months, and then there he'd be at the door with a big smile and gifts that he thought would make up for the time he'd been away. Spring had always been so thrilled with those gifts. She'd treasured them long after he'd left. But now she realized those cheap toys and knickknacks could never replace a father.

And neither would one camping trip.

"I'm sorry, but I can't go camping with you, Daddy," she said.

Holt sat up. "Is this because I didn't call you back? I had an emergency come up that I couldn't ignore, Spring-a-ling."

She'd always hated her father's nickname for her. It sounded too much like ding-a-ling. Of course, she had been a ding-a-ling to believe that Holt had turned over a new leaf. If she were Summer, she'd give him hell for showing up unannounced and expecting her to drop everything and go camping with him. But if she were Summer, she never would've gone to see Holt in the first place and been suckered into buying a trailer. But she wasn't Summer, and she couldn't bring herself to be mean to him. Regardless of all his faults, he was her father.

"You should've called me back," she said. "If you had, I would've told you that I just got a job and can't leave without giving notice."

"Sure you can. I do it all the time." He finished off his beer. "Now let's hitch the trailer up to your car and get out of here. I thought we'd stop by to see a friend of mine before we head to Mexico to do a little fishin'." When she didn't move, he squinted through the smoke at her. "Hey, you don't look so good. Did you forget to put on makeup today? Women should always wear makeup. Without it, they look like warmed over death."

"I have makeup on, Daddy. I just don't feel well."

"You must've gotten that weak constitution from your mother. We Hadleys don't get sick." He stood. "Now let's get a move on."

She got annoyed at his insistence. "I'm not getting a move—"

A car door slammed, cutting her off.

Holt immediately ducked and peeked out the window. "Shit." He shoved his cigarette in the opening of the beer can and waved away the smoke. "You don't want to cause a family ruckus, do you, Spring-a-ling? And if that sheriff coming to your door should tell Dirk I'm here, we both know the kind of ruckus that would cause. So it might be best if you didn't mention that your dear ol' daddy came for a visit." He disappeared inside the bathroom.

Spring stared at the bathroom door. Part of her wanted to jerk it open and tell him to get the hell out of her trailer. But the other part knew he was right. If Dirk found out he was there, there would be a ruckus. Not only would Dirk probably go to jail for beating his father senseless, but also Spring didn't want her family knowing how easily she'd been suckered by Holt. So when she answered the knock on the door, she pinned on a big smile and tried to act like her father wasn't hiding in the bathroom and everything was just fine.

Waylon didn't fall for it. As soon as he saw her, his eyes grew concerned. "I gave you the flu."

She shivered as a chill ran through her. "Forgive me if I don't thank you for that gift." She was about to say she needed to get to bed when he stepped up into the trailer and felt her forehead.

"You're burning up." He scooted around her and pulled a blanket off the bed and wrapped it around her shoulders. "Sit down before you fall down." Once she was seated, he sniffed the air. "Have you been smoking?"

She kept her eyes from the bathroom door. "Uhh . . . yeah. I used to smoke, and sometimes a nicotine hit makes me feel better."

He turned to the cupboards and started searching through them. "Nicotine isn't going to make you feel better this time. You need something for the fever, aches, and pains. Do you have any cold medicine?"

"No, but I took some ibuprofen."

He closed the cupboards and turned to her. "That won't work. You need something for all the symptoms. And you'll need plenty of fluids and rest. In fact, why don't I take you to Dirk and Gracie's? You'll be much more comfortable there, and you shouldn't be alone."

She shook her head. "I can't give this to the triplets. Three sick babies are the last thing Dirk and Gracie need. I'll be fine here." About then, her teeth started to chatter.

"You're not fine," he said. "Believe me, I know." He picked up her purse and hooked it over his shoulder before scooping her into his arms.

"What are you doing?" she asked as he moved to the door. "I told you I can't go to Dirk's."

"I'm not taking you to Dirk's." He fumbled with the door handle. "I'm taking you home . . . if I can figure out how to open this damn door."

"I can't go home with you."

He stopped trying to open the door and looked at her. "It's either that or I stay here and take care of you."

She couldn't let him do that. He'd find her father. Besides, if she left with Waylon, hopefully, Holt would give up on the camping idea and leave.

"Fine," she said. "I'll go to your house." She leaned over and jiggled the door handle until it opened. He carried her to his car and seat belted her in as if she were a toddler. She felt too weak to complain. Nor did she complain when they got to his house and he carried her upstairs and deposited her in the bed of his guest room.

"Are you sure you want to do this?" she asked. "People might've overlooked the first time, but they won't overlook this time. There will be gos sip."

He slipped off her high heels. "Let me worry about that. You need to get some rest." He placed her shoes on the floor, then helped her get under the covers and tucked her in. "I'll bring you some hot tea and cold medicine."

"No NyQuil."

He grinned, his green eyes twinkling with humor. "What? Are you afraid you might kiss me?"

That was exactly what she was afraid of. And she wasn't just worried about kissing him. She was worried about giving into the fantasy she'd been having since kissing him. A fantasy that included stripping him naked and ravishing every inch of his studly sheriff's body. But she wasn't about to let him know that.

"In your dreams," she said.

His smile faded as his gaze lowered to her mouth. "Yes. And much too often lately." Before her feverish brain could figure out what he meant, he turned and walked out of the room.

Her headache and shivering were even worse by the time he returned. He set a tray on the nightstand and sat down on the edge of the bed. He picked up the bottle of NyQuil, then measured some out into the little plastic cup and held it out. "I promise I won't let you do anything we'll both regret later."

"No kisses?"

"No kisses."

She took the cup and drank the medicine. After she finished, he handed her a glass of water to help wash it down, then he tucked the covers back around her and picked up a book from the tray.

"Chapter one," he read. "Down the Rab-bit-Hole."

CHAPTER FOURTEEN

THE TAP ON HIS OFFICE door pulled Waylon's attention away from the window. Spring stood in the doorway. She'd recovered from the flu, and he had to admit he was glad to have her back at the office. Things hadn't run smoothly the two days she'd been gone. He'd had to drink his own coffee, deal with all the emails and reports, and answer all the phone calls. And people were extremely disappointed when he answered the phone. They didn't want him helping them with their problems. They wanted Spring. Even Tucker and Jonas moped around like they'd lost their best friend.

It seemed that Spring was now as indispensable as Gail.

And prettier. Much prettier.

Today, she wore white tailored pants that hugged her long legs and a lime-green sweater with a daisy print scarf draped between the sweet hills of her breasts. She'd gotten a haircut. The blue stripe was almost gone, and feathery wisps of ebony hair framed her twilight-blue eyes, high cheekbones,

and full lips she had painted a dew-drenched rasp-
berry. He loved raspberries.

She cleared her throat, and he dragged his attention away from her mouth.

"Yes, Miss Hadley?" It was probably ridiculous
to keep using her surname. Especially when they'd
slept together—or not together as much as in the
same house. But he hoped the proper title would
keep his mind from straying down paths it had no
business straying down. And obviously Spring felt
the same way. She still called him Sheriff Kendall.
Even after he'd nursed her back to health with cold
medicine, hot tea, and *Alice in Wonderland*.

"Sorry to interrupt your work, Sheriff Kendall,"
she said. He hadn't been working. He'd been staring out the window daydreaming about her in his
bathtub. Or maybe fantasizing would be a better
word. Especially when he'd been in the bathtub
with her. And there had been kisses. Lots and lots
of kisses. "Raff Arrington just called," she continued. "And he wanted me to remind you that the
first high school baseball game is this afternoon.
He said he tried calling you, but you didn't answer."

Waylon checked his front pockets, neither of his
phones were there. He must've left them in the
SUV when he went out on patrol at noon. Which
wasn't like him. He might leave his personal phone,
but he never went anywhere without his work
phone. He glanced up to find Spring looking just
as surprised as he was.

"Are you okay?" she asked.

"I'm fine. Why?"

"You've just been acting differently the last few
days . . . nicer." She glanced down at his desk. "And

messier."

His desk wasn't as neat as it usually was. He no longer used a coaster and coffee rings covered his desk calendar—along with a few cinnamon swirl muffin crumbs. His pens weren't lined up. His stapler was nowhere to be found. And his computer screen still had three dancing pugs in pink tutus. It looked nothing like his father's desk had looked. And Waylon realized he was okay with that. He was also okay with taking the rest of the day off and heading to the baseball field.

"Do you like baseball, Miss Hadley?" he asked as he got to his feet.

She seemed confused by the sudden change of subjects. "Not really. The one time I sat down to watch it, I was bored silly."

"Bored? Obviously, you don't understand the game. Baseball is one of the most exciting sports ever invented." He took her arm. "And I'll prove it to you."

"But who is going to stay and answer the phones?"

"There won't be a soul calling. The entire town will be at the game."

He was right. The bleachers at the baseball field were packed with popcorn and sunflower seed munching fans. Fortunately, Raff had saved a couple of seats in the first row. On the way over, they passed Emmett and Joanna. Both were all decked out in Bliss Bobcat t-shirts and caps.

"Hey, Sheriff." Emmett greeted him with a big

grin. "Sure a nice day for a ball game."

"It certainly is." Joanna's gaze swept over to Spring, and she smiled as widely as her husband. "And don't you look lovely today, Spring?"

The sunbonnet next to Joanna tipped up, revealing Ms. Marble's piercing blue eyes. "I'm glad to see you both survived that nasty flu." Her eyes twinkled. "But of course, you had good nurses."

Waylon knew she and Joanna had known about Spring taking care of him, but he hadn't thought they knew about him taking care of Spring. Obviously, the two women knew everything that went on in the town. He could only hope that they also knew how to keep a secret. He might've decided to stop following in his father's footsteps and become his own man. But he didn't want the town thinking that their sheriff was doing naughty things with his assistant. So when they reached the seats Raff had saved, he made sure to sit on one side of Raff and let Spring sit on Raff's other side next to Savannah.

"How come you didn't get a little higher up?" he asked Raff as he sat down. "We'll have trouble seeing the outfield from here."

Raff cast a quick glance at Savannah, who was making a fuss over Spring's scarf. "Bleacher steps are dangerous. I didn't want anyone tripping." Waylon thought Savannah hadn't been listening, but he was wrong. She stopped talking with Spring and turned to Raff.

"I realize you're scared, honey. But you really need to get a grip. I'm a big healthy southern woman. I'm going to be fine. And the baby's going to be fine too." She patted his arm. "Now go get me a large popcorn and a Butterfinger."

While Raff took off for the concession stand, Waylon decided to stay and try to explain the basics of baseball to Spring and Savannah. Neither woman was interested. They were more interested in chatting about everything from designer handbags to designer shoes. And Waylon was relieved when Raff got back.

"They didn't have Butterfingers so I had to get you a Snickers." He sat down on the other side of Savannah, scooting Spring closer to Waylon. So much for trying to make things look completely innocent. It now looked like they were on a double date with Savannah and Raff.

Raff handed Spring a box of popcorn, and she held it out to Waylon. Since he loved popcorn, he couldn't decline. As they sat there munching popcorn and talking with Savannah and Raff, he decided that he didn't care what people might think. The popcorn was buttery. The sunshine warm. And the company good. For the first time in a long time, he was enjoying life.

But he grew a little nervous when the players took the field. Luke had been working hard—not only at practice, but also with Waylon. Waylon could only hope that it had paid off and the coach would play him, even if only for one inning.

They didn't play Luke in the first five innings, but he came out in the sixth.

"There he is!" Savannah grabbed onto Raff's arm. "Oh, doesn't he look so cute in his uniform?"

"Cute?" Raff stared at his wife. "Athletes don't want to look cute, sweetheart. They want to look studly."

She sent him a sly smile. "I bet you were studly in your football uniform."

"Of course." He kissed her. "Now quit flirting with me and let me watch Luke play."

Luke didn't get to pitch. But he did a hell of a job playing center field. He caught a pop fly and made a double play with a ground ball past second that had Waylon jumping to his feet and hollering his approval. Waylon did the same thing when the Bobcats won five to three.

He didn't think anything about his yelling, but the townsfolk seemed to. As the crowd was dispersing, everyone was smiling at him as if he'd thwarted a bank robbery and more than a few men thumped him on the back and said "Glad you enjoyed the game, Sheriff."

On the way back to the office to take Spring to her car, Waylon couldn't help wondering out loud about the town's reaction. "You would've thought that I'd never enjoyed a baseball game before."

Spring glanced over at him. "Have you?"

"Of course I have. I loved baseball growing up. I haven't been to games in the last couple years because I've been concentrating on my job. And right after I got out of college, I didn't go to games because I was pretty depressed about my injury and losing out on the draft. But I loved going to games as a kid." As soon as the words were out, he realized the truth. "I guess I haven't enjoyed a game in a long time." He pulled into the parking lot next to his office. "Where did you park your Jeep?"

"Umm . . . it broke down again and I had to borrow a ranch truck from Dirk."

He glanced over at her. "Did you drop it off at

Emmett's? I'm sure he won't charge you for fixing it again."

"Not yet, but I will." She reached for the door handle. "Well, thanks for inviting me to the game. It was fun."

He lifted an eyebrow. "Fun? Every time I looked over, you and Savannah were talking."

"Which was why it was so much fun."

He smiled, and her gaze lowered to his mouth. Without any warning, she reached out and brushed her thumb over his bottom lip. Heat sizzled through him like a wildfire, and he caught her wrist. Her eyes were wide, but not innocent. They held the same heat that spiraled through him.

"Popcorn butter," she whispered.

He should've released her hand and left it at that. But he couldn't. He lifted her hand to his lips and gently sucked on the pad of her thumb. Her breath came out in a startled whoosh, but she didn't pull away. In fact, she drew closer, her eyelids drooping and her lips parting. He knew he was playing with fire, but he didn't care. He released her hand and slid his fingers around her jaw, tilting her chin up for his kiss. He was a puff of breath away from her delectable lips when his phone rang.

Not his personal phone, but his business one.

He closed his eyes and took a deep breath before he released Spring and answered it. "Sheriff Kendall."

"Hey, Waylon. It's Sheriff Davis over in Malcolm County. I was hoping you could do me a favor and keep a lookout for someone."

Waylon cleared the desire from his throat. "Sure thing, Mike. Who am I keeping a lookout for?"

"Holt Hadley."

Waylon glanced over at Spring, but she didn't seem to be listening. Still, he opened the door and got out before he continued the conversation. "What did he do?"

"It seems he's been running an illegal gambling hall on a used RV lot. When we raided the place, we found RVs filled with slot machines and black-jack and poker tables. What we didn't find was Holt. My guess is that he got tipped off and headed to Mexico, but there's a chance he could be hiding out with family. I've checked with one of his daughters in Houston and his mother-in-law in Waco. None of them have seen hide nor hair of him, and from the sounds of it, they don't want to. That only leaves his son. And since you know Dirk, I thought you could talk to him and see if he's heard from his father."

Waylon wasn't surprised to find out Holt Hadley was running a gambling racket. He'd only met the man once, but he'd known immediately that Holt wasn't a model citizen.

"Holt certainly isn't on the most wanted list," the sheriff continued. "But these gambling halls are cropping up all over the place and the governor wants to put a stop to them by coming down hard on the people running them. It would look good if I could bring him in."

"Sure. I'll see what I can find out and get back to you." After he hung up, he turned to Spring, who had gotten out of the car and was standing there watching him.

"Is there a bad criminal on the loose?" she asked.

He started to tell her, but then thought better

of it. No one wanted to hear bad things about their father. Especially a softhearted woman who thought the best of everyone. He would talk to Dirk. Although he doubted if Dirk had seen Holt. Everyone knew that there was no lost love between the two men.

"Nothing to worry about," he said.

She studied him for a moment before she lowered her gaze. "Listen, I want to apologize for . . . touching you. Butter or no butter, that wasn't professional."

He didn't know why the apology annoyed him. Maybe because he wanted Spring to touch him. And he wanted to touch her. Which was crazy. He was the sheriff. If anyone needed to be professional, he did.

"I haven't been acting very professional either. I had no business bringing you back to my house and taking care of you. I should've asked Joanna to take care of you. Or Ms. Marble."

She lifted her gaze. "Ms. Marble wouldn't have helped. I think she's trying to get us together."

He shook his head. "I should've known she was up to matchmaking. She's been responsible for more than a few weddings in this town. She doesn't realize that I'm not interested in getting married." He paused. "But I have come to realize that I am in need of female companionship." In a bad way. "It's just not a good idea for that companion to be someone I work with."

"I couldn't agree more," she said a little too quickly.

He studied her pretty pink mouth. "It's totally against office policy."

She stared at his mouth. "Totally."

"So we're in agreement that a . . . personal relationship between us is a bad idea."

"In complete agreement." She held out her hand as if they were making a pact. And in a way, they were.

He took her hand. It was soft, but with an underlying strength that he'd come to admire. "I'll see you tomorrow, Miss Hadley."

They held hands and stared into one another's eyes for a little longer than was probably necessary, but danged if Waylon could look away . . . or let her go. It was Spring who finally pulled her hand free and walked away. But she stopped before she reached her truck and turned. "Thank you for taking me to the baseball game. I did have fun."

Waylon had had fun too. Too much fun.

"You're welcome." He waited until she had gotten in her truck and pulled away before he climbed in his SUV. He should've gone home. Sherlock was waiting for dinner. Instead, he sat there and thought about the heated brush of her thumb against his bottom lip. And her desire-filled blue eyes. And the longing that still gnawed at his insides. A longing he needed to take care of with someone other than the woman who worked for him.

He pulled out his personal phone and tapped the online dating app. He scrolled through the messages until he found Lynn's latest message. It had come in while he'd been at the baseball game. He ignored the conversation topic they had started about what pains in the butts younger siblings could be and typed a one-line question.

Would you like to meet?

CHAPTER FIFTEEN

"**I** CAN'T THANK YOU ENOUGH FOR hooking me up with Mrs. Miller," Gracie said as she spooned rice cereal and peaches into Luana's mouth. "She's watched the girls four times now and is wonderful with them."

"You're helping her out as much as she's helping you." Spring tried to feed Luella a spoonful of rice cereal and peaches, but her niece kept turning her head away from the spoon. "She has been so lonely since her kids and grandkids moved away. The triplets have filled that lonely space."

"Well, it's working out perfectly. Thanks to you." Gracie spooned in another bite. "I'm also glad you decided to move back into the guest room. It's nice to have a female to talk to that can answer with more than one syllable."

Spring liked spending time with Gracie too. But she missed living on her own. For the first time in her life, she'd been able to do what she wanted to do. She'd listened to her music as loudly as she wanted without Summer yelling at her to turn it down. She'd eaten junk food without Autumn cautioning her on all the preservatives she was putting in her body. The trailer might've been the size of a postage stamp with a showerhead that dribbled rather than sprayed, but it had been all hers. And she missed it . . . she also missed her Jeep.

Her father had stolen both the night Waylon showed up. Or not stolen exactly. Holt had called her the next day when she was recuperating at Waylon's and told her he had "borrowed" them. Since she couldn't leave her job, he didn't think she'd mind if he did a little camping on his own. His actions showed such disrespect for her that there was no way to justify it. It was the pin that finally busted the fairytale bubble she'd been living in. Her father hadn't changed, and he wasn't going to. The only reason he'd called her and been so nice is because he wanted to con her into buying a trailer she didn't even want. And now he had taken that trailer and left her feeling like a gullible idiot.

Which was probably why she didn't want to tell her family what had happened. She'd been work-ing so hard to prove she was a responsible adult, and yet, she'd let Holt get the best of her. If her family found out, it would only confirm that she was an irresponsible ditz. So she'd lied about her Jeep breaking down again and wanting to move back in with Dirk because she couldn't take the trailer's weak water pressure. She could only pray that Holt brought her trailer and Jeep back before anyone figured it out.

"I enjoy talking to you too," she said to Gracie. "And hanging with my nieces. Although I'm not very good at getting them to eat." She tried to give Luella another bite, but the baby refused with a jerk of her head.

"Luella does the same thing with me. She prefers to feed herself." Gracie pulled a breakfast wafer from the box on the kitchen table and handed it to Luella. The baby squealed with delight before ramming the wafer into her mouth and gnawing on it with her front teeth.

Spring picked up Lucinda's spoon. Her niece immediately opened her mouth like a little baby bird. But a few bites later, she decided she was finished and spit the entire mouthful of rice cereal and peaches right at Spring.

Spring laughed as she wiped a glob from her eye. "It's a good thing I haven't gotten ready for work yet." She glanced at the clock on the stove. "Although I better get going. Sheriff Kendall gets grumpy if he doesn't get his coffee first thing in the morning."

Gracie handed her a napkin. "Is that what's changed our sheriff? Your coffee?" When Spring sent her a surprised look, she elaborated. "Ever since Waylon became sheriff, he's been a real grump. But when he came into the diner the other day, he seemed like the Waylon I knew growing up. He stopped at each table to chat with people about the high school baseball team and the nice weather. He even did a little flirting with the Sanders sisters."

"Maybe he was just having a good day."

"Or maybe his life has been brightened by some Spring sunshine." Gracie sent her a knowing look. "It seems like too much of a coincidence that he got happy after you started working for him. And I can't help but wonder if there's not something more going on between you and our sheriff."

There *was* something going on between her and Waylon. It was called lust. What happened after the baseball game was a perfect example. She shouldn't have touched him. One brush of his lips had brought back all the desire she felt when he'd kissed her. At that moment, she had never wanted anyone as much as she had wanted Waylon. As much as she still wanted Waylon.

She wiped off Lucinda's mouth. "There's nothing going on between me and Way—Sheriff Kendall. We just work together."

"But you can't tell me that you don't think he's hot."

No, Spring couldn't say that. Waylon was hot, and it seemed like he was getting hotter by the day. It was his smiles. When Waylon smiled, he went from handsome to sizzling in two seconds flat. And Gracie was right. He was smiling a lot more lately. He smiled every time Spring brought him his morning cup of coffee. He smiled when Mrs. Miller had brought in her cat's kittens for Spring to meet. And the other day, she'd caught him smiling at his dancing pug screensaver.

She walked around the office in a constant state of arousal.

"Who's hot?" Dirk strode into the room with a scowl on his face.

Gracie tipped her lips up for a kiss. "You are, sweetheart."

He leaned down and kissed her. "Damn straight." He glanced at Spring. "You have something in your hair."

"Your daughter gave me a cereal and peaches shower," Spring said.

Dirk grinned before he leaned down to kiss Lucinda's head. "Good girl. You keep your auntie humble. She's always been a little too big for her britches."

"I think that's Auntie Summer you're talking about." She smiled at Lucinda. "Your Auntie Spring is perfect. Just like you." She gave her an air kiss that made Lucinda giggle. Then she did the same for each niece until they squealed and chortled.

Dirk ruffled Spring's hair. "You are pretty perfect." He sat down at the table, and his expression turned serious. "And I'm proud of you. From what I've heard, you're doing a bang-up job for the sheriff. Everyone in town thinks so." He paused. "And if you still need that loan, it's yours. Although I think you should spend it on a new vehicle. The Jeep is crap. I also hope you don't take off too soon. I've gotten used to having my sister around."

She wished she could take off. Maybe some distance from Waylon would cure her infatuation. Unfortunately, she couldn't leave now without everyone finding out about her father borrowing her trailer. Plus, she couldn't leave Waylon. He had come to depend on her, and as much as he made her weak-kneed and loopy, she couldn't let him down. Nor could she leave Mrs. Miller without someone to chat with about her cats and grandkids. Or Jonas without someone to talk to about his late wife. And she'd promised Tucker a dance at the spring dance.

"Thanks for the offer." She got up. "But it would be irresponsible to take a loan from my baby brother." She sent him a sassy wink as she headed to the guest room to get ready for work.

It turned out to be one of those days when nothing seemed to go right. She ran out of mousse so her hair looked flat. The shirt she wanted to wear was wrinkled and she didn't have time to iron it. On the way to work, she tried to call her father, but he didn't answer. When she got to the office, Waylon wasn't there and the coffee machine was broken. Then her computer froze up so she couldn't answer emails.

Heaving a frustrated sigh, she got up from her desk and treated herself to a bag of peanut M&M's. Once she had some chocolate in her, she unlocked Waylon's office so she could answer emails on his computer.

It looked like he'd been in before she'd gotten there. His computer was on and his personal laptop open. It was merely an accident the she brushed against it when she sat down. The online dating screen popped up, and it looked like the revisions she'd made to his profile page had worked. He had gotten more than a few "hugs" and his message board was full of messages.

Spring popped the last of the M&M's in her mouth and glanced at the open door. It wasn't like she was snooping. He'd left his laptop open for anyone to see. The fact that he'd locked his door was pushed to the back of her mind as she read the messages. Most were from a woman named Lynn. As she read on, she realized that Waylon and Lynn had really hit it off. They talked about everything from family to their favorite flavors of ice cream. Spring didn't know why she felt so hurt. Maybe because she'd been working for him for over a month now and he had never told her the things he'd told Lynn.

Spring didn't know how much he missed his family and how lonely his big house felt. She didn't know that his favorite ice cream wasn't ice cream at all but rainbow sherbet. Or that he didn't like fishing but loved to hunt. And she certainly didn't know that he couldn't wait for his assistant to get back so he wouldn't have to deal with the new temp.

Spring crinkled the empty bag of M&M's in her fist and blinked back her tears. She shouldn't take it personally. Hadn't she just wished that she could take off? She shouldn't be hurt that Waylon felt the same way. But she did feel hurt. And when she read about Waylon and Lynn meeting, she felt even more hurt . . . and mad. He had asked Lynn to meet him the same day he had taken Spring to the baseball game. Right after he'd almost kissed her.

She clicked on Lynn's profile page wanting to see what the woman that had captured Waylon's attention looked like, but Lynn didn't have a picture of herself. She had a picture of a dog. Which probably meant she was as ugly as a mud fence. And she wasn't funny either. Waylon hadn't typed one LOL in all of the messages. Not one. And he'd LOLed plenty of times with Spring.

"Did you get a promotion I wasn't aware of?"

She jumped guiltily and turned to find Waylon standing in the doorway. His hair was mussed from the spring winds, and he was smiling. Her heart added another beat. She couldn't help but wonder if Lynn's heart would beat faster when she met Waylon.

"Where have you been?" she snapped.

His eyebrows lifted beneath the tipped-up brim of his cowboy hat. "Excuse me?"

"If you're going to leave the office, you should let me know where you're going."

He smiled. "Yes, ma'am." He held up two to-go cups. "But the coffee machine was broken and I thought I'd go to the diner for our morning coffee. Then Stella talked me into some pancakes and I got to talking with Emmett about baseball and completely lost track of the time." He walked over and placed one cup on the desk. "Disgustingly sugared and flavored." He sat down in the chair across from her and took a sip from his cup. She thought he was going to get after her for being in his office. He didn't.

"So do you want to tell me what bee has gotten into your bonnet?" he asked.

"There's no bee. Can't a person have a bad day?"

He squinted one eye at her. "Not a person named Spring."

She lifted her chin. "Miss Hadley to you."

He tipped back his head and laughed. She should've felt smug that she could make him laugh when Lynn couldn't. But instead she felt even more hurt. Spring now knew the reason for Waylon's abrupt personality change. He had found a match. A perfect match who might not make him laugh, but made him smile.

She picked up her cup and stood. "Thank you for the coffee. Now if you'll excuse me, I have work to do."

Before she reached the door, he spoke in a deep timbre that had warmth settling in her stomach. "I hope your day gets better, Miss Hadley."

Her day didn't get better. It got worse as the morning wore on. She couldn't stop thinking about Waylon and Lynn. And when Joanna Daily called and asked her to help decorate for the spring dance she decided it was time to leave town. She'd have to come clean about her trailer and Jeep, but she didn't care anymore if her family thought she was a gullible ditz. All she cared about was Waylon finding a perfect match.

"I'm sorry, but I won't be here for the dance."

"You won't?" Joanna said. "Did Gail call and say she was coming back? Last time I talked with her, her mother still wasn't doing well."

"It's not that," Spring said. "I only planned to work here temporarily. Just until I got enough money to fix my Jeep."

There was a long pause before Joanna spoke. "Well, Emmett mentioned you still had a little to pay on the Jeep. And I'm sure you're not the type of person to leave unpaid bills. Besides, the dance is only a week away."

She tried to think of another excuse why she had to leave, but she couldn't think of one. She certainly couldn't tell Joanna Daily it was because she had major hots for the sheriff and was jealous that he'd found a girlfriend who made him smile.

"Fine," she said. "I'll stay until after the dance." She hung up the phone a little harder than she'd intended.

"I'm going to make a guess and say that your day hasn't gotten better."

She glanced up to see Waylon standing in the doorway of his office. "If you want lunch from the diner, you'll have to get it yourself. I'm too backed up to order you lunch."

He pulled on his hat and smiled. "No need. I'm meeting someone for lunch."

"At the diner?"

"Uhh . . . no." A blush stained his cheeks. "Did you want me to bring you something?"

As she studied his guilty-looking face, it dawned on her who he was having lunch with. Lynn. He was meeting Lynn. They had talked about meeting for lunch in the messages. Waylon had just interrupted her before she got to the exact date and time. But it was today. Now.

"No," she said. "I don't want anything."

He nodded. "Then I'll see you after lunch." He walked out.

Spring stared at the glass doors for only a moment before she grabbed her purse. By the time she locked up and got to the parking lot, Waylon's sheriff's SUV was already gone. She caught up with it right outside of Bliss and tailed him all the way to a truck stop a good twenty minutes out of town.

Leave it to a man to pick a truck stop as a first date meeting place. This would probably be strike one for poor Waylon. There was only one woman Spring knew who enjoyed eating at truck stops.

She parked in between two semis so he wouldn't spot her and watched as he got out of his SUV. If she knew him at all, he was early for the date. The woman would no doubt show up closer to noon. But only a few moments later, a red Mustang pulled into the parking lot and parked only a couple spaces away from Waylon's.

A red Mustang that Spring recognized immediately. She also recognized the face of the beautiful, dark-haired woman who climbed out of the car.

It was the same face Spring saw every day when she looked in the mirror.

CHAPTER SIXTEEN

WAYLON DIDN'T NOTICE THAT HIS date had arrived. He was too busy watching Spring. She would make a horrible undercover cop. He had spotted Dirk's truck tailing him before he even left Bliss. And he knew why she was tailing him. It was obvious when he'd walked into his office that she'd been reading his messages to Lynn and had found out about their meeting. Her blue eyes had snapped with anger and jealousy.

Spring being jealous shouldn't make him happy. Her developing feelings for him complicated things. But damned if he didn't feel downright joyful. Even now, he was sitting there smiling like an idiot as he watched her through the window. She seemed to be staring at something intently. Then she seemed to be talking to herself. Or more like yelling. He wasn't a lip reader, but he knew cuss words when he saw them.

He realized why she was cussing when a woman swept past his line of view. She wore those athletic clothes women liked to wear everywhere—a form-fitting tank top, black spandex pants, and running shoes. She had a nice body, but it was a little too toned for Waylon's taste. He liked his women softer. He glanced back at Spring, but the truck was gone.

His smile faded, along with his happy mood.

The restaurant door opened. For a second, he thought that Spring had parked somewhere else and decided to come in. But then he realized that the woman who walked in the door was the same woman in the athletic wear. A woman who looked exactly like Spring, but with longer hair she had pulled back in a ponytail.

What was Spring's sister doing in a truck stop?

He got his answer when she glanced around and her gaze locked with his. She waved and then strode straight toward him with purpose. When she reached the booth, she didn't wait for an invitation before she slid in across from him.

"Sorry, I'm late. Autumn was not happy when she found out what I'd done, and we had a big blow out." She held out a hand. "Summer Lynn Hadley."

He was so stunned all he could do was stare. On closer inspection, she didn't look that much like her sister. Her eyes weren't as sparkly or her hair as cute . . . or her lips as kissable.

"I understand why you're surprised," Summer said. "And I'm sorry I had to meet you under false pretenses. But if you had known who I was, I don't think you would've been as open and honest with me. And I needed to know the type of man my little sister was working for." She took the menu he'd been looking at and closed it. "You don't need that. You want their cheeseburgers. I made my sisters stop here on the way back from Dirk's wedding, and this place has dynamite cheeseburgers."

It took a moment for Waylon to catch up. "You mean you joined the online dating site to find out the type of man your sister was working for?"

She tucked the menu behind the sugar and napkin dispensers. "Isn't that what I just said? And after working with her for weeks, you should understand why. My sister is gullible. Over the years, she's fallen prey to all kinds of assholes that I've had to scare off. Men who want to take advantage of her innocence and sweet disposition. She's like a magnet for creeps and losers. I wasn't about to let her work for some horny sheriff who only hired her so he could boink her on his desk."

He wanted to be offended, but lately he'd felt like a horny sheriff who desperately wanted to boink Spring on his desk . . . or in the guest room of his house . . . or in his SUV. He remained silent as she continued.

"So when Autumn told me about Spring helping you with your online dating, I figured that was my opportunity to see what kind of man you were." She studied him. "Turns out you're a pretty decent guy who cares about his family, his dog, and the people of his town. If I wasn't so busy with the store, I might think about dating you."

Summer was pretty, but he felt absolutely nothing when he looked at her. No flash of heat. No zing of desire. She didn't make him want to pull her into his arms and kiss her senseless.

Her cellphone pinged, and she pulled it out of her purse and checked it. She must not have liked the text she'd received because her lips tilted in a frown. "Damn you, Ryker." She stared at her phone for a second before she typed a reply that had her frown turning into a smile. A rather evil smile. Then she put her cellphone back in her purse and looked at Waylon. "Sorry for the interruption. Business."

Somehow Waylon doubted that.

She lifted a hand and waved the waitress over, then proceeded to order for both of them. "We'll take two cheeseburgers medium with no onions and extra crispy fries. And two Dr Peppers. No ice in one. And be sure to go heavy on the mayo on one of those burgers."

Waylon now understood why Spring had left Houston. It had to be tough working with someone as controlling and domineering as Summer. Before the waitress could finish writing down the order, he corrected it. "Make mine a plain hamburger medium well with onions. And water is fine for me."

Summer waited for the waitress to walk off before she lifted an eyebrow at him. "Don't like women ordering for you, huh?"

"Your sister orders lunch for me every day, but she always asks me what I want first."

Summer shrugged. "That's Spring for you. She likes to make people happy. Which is what gets her in trouble. The bum who lived in the alley behind our store is a perfect example. Spring was so busy running back inside to get a hundred-dollar sweater to give to him so he wouldn't be cold, she forgot to lock up thousands of dollars of merchandise."

Waylon had wondered what had caused Spring to leave Houston. Now he knew. It made sense.

Spring was the type of person who always put other people's needs before her own. She never got frustrated with Mrs. Miller. Or with Jonas or Tucker. She was kind to a fault. And suddenly he realized there was no fault in being kind. He smiled at the thought of Spring giving an old bum a designer sweater to keep warm.

Summer scowled. "It's not funny. She could've bankrupted us."

"But she didn't."

She released her breath. "No, but she could've. And I had every right to get pissed. I've been working my butt off trying to make sure we don't lose the store, and then Spring pulled that stunt. Sometimes she can be so ditzy."

Waylon didn't know why his hackles got up. He'd called his little brothers much worse. It was a sibling's right to call each other names. Still, he couldn't help defending Spring. "She's not ditzy. She just gets distracted easily. Usually by something that's important. And keeping a homeless person warm is important. While she's worked for me, she's brightened everyone's lives in one way or the other." He paused. "Including mine."

Summer studied him for a long moment. "You obviously are more infatuated with Spring than I thought." Her eyes narrowed. "Have you boinked my sister?"

"No!" he said so adamantly and loudly that the truck drivers sitting at the bar turned and looked at him. He lowered his voice. "I did not have sex with your sister. She's just my employee . . . and my friend." The last words just popped out, but he realized their truth as soon as they did. Somewhere amid the morning coffee, daily teasing, and flu nursing, they'd become friends. He had wanted a female companion, and Spring fit nicely into that slot. She was funny, smart, and honest. And he trusted her not to gossip about him. He also desired her. But he wasn't going to do anything about that desire.

Summer must've believed him because her shoulders relaxed. "Spring makes friends with everyone. It's annoying how easily she makes friends. Customers invite her to their homes for dinner. Professors in college gave her A's just for showing up to class. And she was voted the most popular in high school and never tried out for one thing. Not one."

Waylon was starting to get the picture. "I guess you tried out for everything."

She lowered her gaze and picked at her paper napkin. "Class president. Head cheerleader. Captain of the softball team." She paused. "But I worked my butt off for everything I got. All Spring had to do was smile."

"Which made you resentful."

Her gaze snapped up. "Hell yeah, I was resentful. I'm still resentful. I'm resentful that my little sister dances through life wearing rose-colored glasses while Autumn and I have all the work and stress. She never once worried about the store going bankrupt and only offered a measly sorry when she forgot to lock the door. Then she gets her feeling hurt and spends all her money on a stupid travel trailer and runs off without a word."

She glanced around. "I don't know what I'm doing here. If she wants to run off in a stupid vintage trailer, I should let her. It's just that Autumn is upset about Spring being gone. She has this stupid triplet theory that we aren't whole if we're not together. I don't think that, of course. I'm fine without Spring."

She protested a little too much. She missed Spring. It was there in her eyes when she spoke about her sister.

The waitress showed up with their food, and Waylon waited until she left before he spoke. "It's not easy being the oldest. The responsibility gene that comes with the title isn't fun. I still worry about my little brothers and they're married with families of their own. It's just part of loving them."

She sighed. "I shouldn't give a damn. I should let her live her sunshine daisy life and see where it gets her."

He put mustard on his hamburger bun. "So is that why you wanted to meet today? You want me to try to talk Spring into coming back to Houston?"

She picked up a French fry and munched on it. "It was a stupid idea. Spring is as stubborn as the day is long. Once she gets something in her head, there's no getting it out. And she seems to want to prove she can make it without us."

"Is that what you're worried about? Spring making it without you and Autumn?" Before she could reply, he continued. "I get that you three are close. I'm close to my brothers and we didn't share the same womb. But we knew when it was time to let go and let each other live our own lives."

Her blue eyes turned angry. "Spring isn't ready to be let go. She's too immature. She's a baby bird who isn't ready to fly."

"The Spring you describe and the Spring who works for me sound like two different people. My Spring seems to be flying just fine and has no problem taking responsibility. She answers most of my emails, fields all my phone calls, and keeps the office running smoothly while I'm away. I trust her with my files and to lock up the office. And I trust her to distinguish between an emergency and a little old woman who just needs company. She's capable, dependable, and hardworking."

Summer studied him. "Obviously, she's hoodwinked you. So I take it that you're not going to talk her into coming back to Houston?"

"No. If you want her to come back, you'll have to talk to her yourself."

Her forehead knotted. "I can't. I promised Granny Bon I would leave her alone. She thinks I've been suffocating Spring."

So that was why she'd wanted to meet outside of Bliss? She didn't want anyone seeing her and reporting back to Granny Bon. He wondered if he should tell her about Spring being there, but then decided he didn't want to open up that can of worms. He agreed with Granny Bon. Summer was suffocating. The lengths she'd gone to said it all. He should be mad at her for deceiving him on the online dating site, but he wasn't. She might be controlling, but it was obvious that she loved Spring and worried about her.

"Maybe you should listen to Granny Bon, Summer," he said. "Maybe a few months away from each other will be good for you and Spring. And you don't have to worry about her. She has an entire town looking out for her."

"Including you."

He nodded. "Including me."

She studied him for a moment before she shrugged. "I guess I don't have much choice." She picked up her cheeseburger and took a big bite.

For the rest of the lunch, they didn't talk about Spring. Instead, they talked about work and Dirk, Gracie, and the triplets. As with messaging, they seemed to have no trouble conversing. When they finished lunch and he walked her out to her Mustang, she sent him a quizzical look.

"Are you disappointed that I didn't turn out to be the woman of your dreams?"

He wasn't disappointed. In fact, he almost felt relieved. And he figured if he felt like that, he had no business being on a dating site. "I'm not looking for the woman of my dreams. Thanks for lunch, Summer. I'm sure we'll be seeing each other again soon."

"You can count on it, Sheriff. I'll honor my promise to my grandmother. But if Spring isn't back in a month, I'll be coming to get her." She climbed into her car and gave him a brief wave. Then with no regard to his profession, she backed out and peeled out of the parking lot.

Waylon watched her go, and one thought stuck in his head. A month. He only had one more month with Spring.

It didn't seem like nearly enough time.

CHAPTER SEVENTEEN

SUMMER.

Waylon's online girlfriend was her sister.

Spring still couldn't believe it. She couldn't believe that fate would be so cruel as to pair together her main infatuation and her meanie sister on an online dating site. But that's exactly what had happened. And she shouldn't be surprised. They made a perfect couple. They both enjoyed being the boss, control, and working themselves to an early grave.

Still, it wasn't fair.

Spring had first dibs on Waylon. And there was a first-come-first-serve rule between the three sisters. Of course, Spring hadn't exactly called dibs. Whenever Spring talked with her family members, she acted like Waylon was just her boss.

But he was more than that. She didn't realize how much more until she read his messages to her sister. Each word had felt like a punch in the stomach. And that was when she thought it was some faceless woman he was flirting with. Now that she knew it was Summer, she was even more hurt. Which made her come to the realization that she wasn't just sexually attracted to Waylon. She was mentally attracted . . . and even worse, soulfully attracted. She liked him. And she had started to think that he liked her too. Not just the person who hid behind a bright smile, but also the person beneath those bright smiles.

But she'd been wrong.

He liked Summer.

"You look beautiful."

She glanced behind her to see Dirk standing in the doorway of the guest bedroom with a proud brotherly look on his face. She looked back at her reflection in the mirror. She had loved the daisy-print sundress when she'd bought it, now it just looked childish and stupid. "I'm not beautiful," she said. "I'm the cute triplet, remember? Autumn is the beautiful one."

Dirk walked into the room and stood behind her. He placed his hands on her shoulders and studied her reflection. "Okay, what's going on? You've been moping around here for the last few days like your favorite dog has run away. Even my adorable daughters haven't been able to pull a smile out of you. Are you missing Summer and Autumn, is that it?"

She had been missing her sisters, but now she only missed Autumn. She never wanted to see Summer again. But she couldn't tell Dirk that without explaining why.

"I'm fine." She moved over to the dresser and picked up her mascara. "I guess I'm just tired. I've been working long hours at the sheriff's office, and I stayed up late last night helping Joanna Daily with the dance decorations."

He sat down on the bed. "I overheard Joanna and Ms. Marble talking at the diner the other day. Joanna said she hoped that you and Waylon were working things out." Spring almost poked herself in the eye with the mascara wand. "What things was she talking about? Are you two not getting along? I thought you liked working for Waylon."

She put the wand back in the tube. "I do like working for Waylon."

At least she had before she found out that he was dating her sister. Not that a truck stop lunch could be considered dating. But they could've gone out again and Spring just didn't know it. Waylon had spent a lot of time out of the office in the last few days. When he was there, Spring had tried to avoid him as much as possible. She was afraid if they were alone together, her anger over his and Summer's deception would spill out. Then he really would know how much she liked him.

Dirk pointed a finger at her. "That look right there is what I'm talking about. When you're not looking all sad and depressed, you look like you want to kill someone."

She unclenched her jaw and smiled. "You're imagining things, little brother. I don't think you're getting enough sleep at night."

He flopped back on the pillows. "I haven't had a good night's sleep since the triplets were born. Gracie wants to go to the dance tonight, but I'd rather keep Mrs. Miller and just sleep."

"You can't do that. Gracie is really looking forward to the dance. She bought a new dress and boots and has spent most of the day getting ready."

Dirk rubbed a hand over his face. "I know. For the last week, all she's talked about is dancing until past midnight like we did on our wedding night. I just don't know if I can do it."

Spring didn't want to go to the dance either. She would much rather climb into bed and try to pretend that Waylon and Summer getting together was all just a bad dream. But that would be cowardly. And Spring might be ditzy, but she had never been cowardly. She lifted her chin and walked over to the bed.

"Come on, little brother." She took his hands and pulled him into a sitting position. "We Hadleys can do anything we set our minds to. Now go get your wife. We are going to rock the spring dance!"

When she walked into Zane's barn, Spring couldn't help feeling proud of the decorations she'd helped with. The barn looked like it belonged in a country magazine. Strings of clear lights hung from the rafters and reflected off the pretty oak dance floor. Tables were set up on the sides with blue and white checked gingham tablecloths and bales of hay for people to sit on. Vases of bluebonnets graced each table, and the barn doors had been opened wide to let in the star-filled sky.

Spring immediately went to the table in the back where Ms. Marble and Joanna were serving punch and cookies to see if they needed any help.

"We've got this handled," Ms. Marble said. "You go on and enjoy the dancing." She glanced around. "I wonder where the sheriff is. He usually arrives early to town activities."

"Maybe he has a date," Spring said a little too snidely. When both women glanced at her in question, she forced a smile. "I'm sure he'll be here soon."

"Spring!" Tucker came weaving through the crowd toward her. "I was worried you weren't going to show up."

"Of course I showed up. I promised you a dance." As if on cue, the band that had been warming up started to play a Blake Shelton song.

Tucker held out his hand. "Then let's get to it."

Tucker was as enthusiastic at dancing as he was at everything else. He whipped her around the dance floor like they were two of the last competitors in a dance competition. Spring tried to keep up, but her heart just wasn't in it. After two country swings, a line dance, and a polka, she was exhausted and had to beg for a break.

"Sure," Tucker said as he led her off the dance floor. "You want me to go get you some punch?"

"Actually, I think I'd like some air." Once they were outside, she leaned against the side of the barn and looked up at the sky. "It's a beautiful—"

Tucker's lips cut off her words. She tried to push him away, but he kept coming back with wet, sloppy kisses. She finally had to get a little mean. "Stop it, Tucker!"

She shoved him hard enough that he stumbled back into the paddock fence, then slid to his butt. In the moonlight, his face looked confused. Obviously, dancing so many dances with him had led him to believe that there was more to their relationship than there was. She was about to explain

that she only liked him as a friend when Waylon
stepped out of the barn. Spring's heart almost
jumped out of her chest.

"You have a little too much to drink, Tuck?"
Waylon asked as he helped Tucker to his feet.

"No, sir, Sheriff. I was just . . ." Tucker swallowed.
"I was just getting some air with Spring."

Waylon didn't even glance in her direction.
"Looks like you've had enough air."

Tucker nodded before he picked up his hat and
slapped it against his leg. "I guess I'll see you inside,
Spring." He walked away. Since she had no desire
to be alone with Waylon, she quickly went to follow.

Waylon blocked her path. "Everything okay?"

"Yes. I just wanted some fresh air. Tucker thought
I wanted more."

She couldn't see his eyes in the shadow of his hat,
but as always, she felt them. "Come on."

"Come on where?"

"If you want some air, let's go for a walk." He
turned and headed around the paddock to the
open pasture. She didn't have to follow, but she
couldn't stop herself. Nor could she stop herself
from bringing up Summer when she finally caught
up.

"When were you planning on telling me that
you were online dating my sister?"

He glanced over at her, and his white teeth
flashed in the moonlight. "Why would I have to
tell you when you snoop on my laptop and read
all my messages? Or when you follow me on my
lunch date and skulk around watching me?"

Her mouth dropped open, but she quickly

snapped it shut. "You knew?"

"You aren't very good at spying." He took her hand and led her around a pile of cow manure. Once they were clear, he didn't release her. In fact, he linked their fingers and held on tight. She should have tugged her hand free. She didn't.

"I wasn't spying." When he shot a glance over at her, she acquiesced. "Okay, I was spying. But only because you didn't tell me you were messaging someone and I was curious about who she was."

His thumb stroked over the back of her hand, and a shower of tingling heat shot through her like sparkler sparks. "So why are you so mad? I thought you wanted me to find a woman."

She stopped and turned to him. "Not my sister!"

"Hmm? So it's okay for me to date other women. Just not your sisters."

She wanted to say yes, but the word got stuck in the back of her throat. Probably by the image of Waylon being with any woman . . . other than her. When she didn't answer, he pushed.

"Answer the question, Spring."

"No," she said. "It's not okay."

"Why not?"

Knowing she liked Waylon and saying it to him were two different things. She pulled her hand away. "I better get back to the dance." She started back, but Waylon's words stopped her.

"I'm not dating Summer, Spring. I didn't even know who she was until she showed up at the truck stop. She was the one who planned the entire thing."

Spring wasn't surprised. Summer had always been a schemer. But she just couldn't figure out why she had gone to all the trouble. She turned back to him. "But why would she do that?"

"She wanted to make sure her little sister wasn't working for a jerk." He paused. "And she wanted me to talk you into going back to Houston. She misses you."

Spring couldn't have been more shocked. Or happier. She knew her sister would miss her eventually. Her plan had worked. But that wasn't what made her the happiest . . . or the most relieved. Waylon and Summer weren't dating. Although, after reading the messages, they probably should be. It was obvious that they had a lot in common. The only thing standing in their way was Spring.

"But you like her, don't you?" she said. "And I get why. She's smart and dedicated to her job. And she loves sports and knows the difference between a run and a score. And she's organized and focused."

"But can she make coffee?"

"What?"

"Can she make coffee?" He took a few steps closer. He'd taken off his hat, and the streaks of blond in his brown hair glistened in the moonlight like rivers of gold. "And can she help Mrs. Miller find a babysitting job to keep her from getting so lonely? Or help Jonas get through his grieving so he can move on? Can she step into a room and brighten it with just a smile? Or make me laugh when I thought I'd forgotten how?" He took her hand and tugged her closer. "And can she make me burn from the inside out with just the brush of her thumb?"

Spring blinked. "I make you burn?"

"Oh, baby, you set me on fire. And I can't fight

the flames anymore." He lowered his head and kissed her. It was as feverish and intense as the first kiss. But this time, he wasn't drugged. This time, he knew exactly what he was doing. And whom he was doing it with.

"Spring," he whispered as he slid a hand around her waist and pulled her close enough to feel the bulge beneath the fly of his jeans. He hadn't lied. She did make him burn. And she wanted to make him burn even hotter.

She slipped her hands into his hair and took charge of the kiss, molding her lips to his and teasing his mouth with her tongue. They stood in the middle of the road tasting each other like the most decadent of desserts until Waylon finally pulled back and nibbled his way down the side of her neck.

"Come home with me."

She tipped her head, giving him better access to her neck. "What about office policy?"

He nipped on her earlobe. "Fuck office policy." He released her and took her hand, tugging her behind him. His long strides ate up the ground, and she had to jog to keep up with him. When they reached his SUV, she pulled back. "I need to tell Dirk and Gracie. They'll worry if I leave without a word. I'll meet you at your house."

He didn't look happy about it, but he nodded. "Hurry."

When she got inside the barn, she looked around for Gracie and Dirk. She expected to find them on the dance floor. Instead, she found them in a stall at the back of the barn. They were cuddled together on a pile of hay, fast asleep.

"I hope you're not planning on waking them. They look like they could use the sleep."

Spring turned to find Ms. Marble standing there. She was the last person Spring wanted to run into. Ms. Marble had a way of looking right through a person. And if she looked through Spring all she'd see was lust.

"Hi, Ms. Marble," she said. "I wonder if you could let Dirk and Gracie know that I went home." Realizing that they'd be even more worried if they went home and she wasn't there, she added. "To my trailer." Ms. Marble's piercing blue eyes settled on her, and Spring caught herself fidgeting. "I haven't been there in a few days and I want to make sure . . . an armadillo hasn't taken up residence."

An armadillo? If Ms. Marble couldn't read through that hokey story, she wasn't as smart as everyone thought. But if she had seen through the lie, she didn't act like it. She merely smiled.

"Armadillos are squatters. One moved into my gardening shed and I didn't have the heart to make him leave." She glanced at the stall. "I'll be sure to let Dirk and Gracie know that there's no need to worry."

Spring thanked her before she headed for the door. It felt like it took forever to get to Waylon's house. He must've felt the same way. When she pulled up in his driveway, he was standing there waiting for her.

"What took you so long?" he asked as he pulled her out of the truck and into his arms. Somehow she ended up plastered against the door of his truck with her dress and bra rearranged and his mouth on her breast. When he pulled the tip between his lips, heat ricocheted through her and her knees buckled.

He caught her before she slipped to the cement. He swept her up and carried her into the house. He bumped the front door closed with his shoulder, then released Spring in a slow slide down his hard body.

"I like your dress," he muttered against her lips as he gathered the hem in his hands and stripped the dress over her head.

"I like your shirt," she muttered back as she slipped her fingers in the open collar of his shirt. She tugged and the snaps popped open. She slipped her hands inside and ran them over the smooth steel of his muscles. It was something she'd fantasized about for weeks, but the reality was ten times better.

"And I love your body," Waylon voiced her exact thoughts as his hands slid over her back to her butt. He gently caressed her butt cheeks as she traced the rippled ridges of his abdomen. They continued to kiss as their hands explored soft skin and hard muscle.

There were beds upstairs, but they never made it to one. Right there in the foyer, bra and panties were slipped off and jeans and boxers tugged down. She stroked him to a steely need, and he fingered her to a heated blaze. A condom appeared and was rolled on. And with only a hike of her leg and a slight adjustment, Waylon was inside of her.

For a brief second, time seemed to stop. Their hands stilled, their lips froze against each other's, and their breath caught and held. The only things that continued to move were their hearts. One beat. One perfectly harmonized beat. Then Waylon started to move, and the desire they'd been denying took charge and burned out of control.

But long after the sparks had fizzled and Waylon had carried her up to his bed, it was that one synchronized heartbeat that kept her awake.

CHAPTER EIGHTEEN

"**U**GH! YOU WERE RIGHT." SPRING crinkled her cute nose and handed the mug back to him. "That has to be the worst coffee I've ever tasted in my life."

Waylon took a sip and shrugged. "And this is one of my better pots."

"It's disgusting. I don't know how you drink it."

He set the mug on the nightstand. "I wouldn't have had to if you'd taken pity on me and gotten out of bed and made me some."

"I'm not walking down to the kitchen naked. Especially with your dog right there staring at us. It's bad enough that we had sex in front of him."

Waylon glanced over at Sherlock, who for once was wide awake and watching them from beneath droopy eyelids as if he couldn't quite figure out what Spring was doing in Waylon's bed.

He knew how the dog felt.

When he woke up this morning and found Spring cuddled next to him, he'd felt a little confused himself. He had never brought a woman home in his life. As he lay there, he'd tried to figure out what made Spring different from the other girls he'd dated. But before he'd found an answer, she'd woken up. And the question had been shelved as he lost himself in the warmth of her delectable body.

He slipped under the covers and moved closer to that delectable body. "We didn't have sex in front of him. He was sound asleep in the kitchen when you ravished me against the front door."

"Me? You were the one doing the ravishing."

He grinned evilly as he pulled her closer. "And I'd like to ravish you again."

She melted into his kiss for only a few seconds before she pulled back and glanced at the clock. "I have to go. I told Dirk I was going to spend the night in my trailer. If he stops by to check on me and sees that the trailer is—" She cut off abruptly. "Sees that I'm not there, he's going to get worried. Besides, I promised Gracie I'd go to church with her this morning."

"I'm sure Gracie won't mind if you don't show up. And just tell Dirk I called you in to help me with some paperwork." He took a nibble of her soft shoulder. "I have a lot of paperwork that needs your attention, Miss Hadley . . . a lot of paperwork."

"I'm sure you do, Sheriff Kendall," she said in a breathy voice that made him as hard as steel. But before he could put that steel to good use, she stopped him. "But I need to go."

He read the stubborn look in her eyes and released a sigh. "Fine. I'll take you back to Dirk's so you can get ready for church." He rolled to his feet and headed for the bathroom. She appeared in the doorway only a second later with a sheet wrapped around her and trailing the floor.

"You can't take me back to Dirk's. He'll know I lied."

"Then I'll take you back to your trailer."

"No!" She suddenly seemed nervous. "I mean I can just drive myself."

He studied her as a thought hit him. "Are you saying you don't want to spend more time with me, Spring? Are you saying this was a one-night stand?"

She shook her head. "I'm not saying that at all. I'd like to spend a lot more time with you, Waylon."

His shoulders relaxed. "Good. Because I want to spend a lot more time with you too."

She smiled that contagious smile of hers. She had bad bedhead and makeup was smudged under her wide blue eyes. Her lips were puffy from all his kisses and she had whisker burns on her neck . . . and probably between her legs. Looking at her, he felt an overwhelming possessiveness that he had never felt in his life.

The question he'd been thinking about earlier that morning came back to him. What made Spring different from the other girls he'd dated? Was it the way she brightened up a room with just a smile? Or her quirky sense of humor? Or her beautiful blue eyes that hid nothing? Or her delectable body? Or her caring nature?

He realized he was staring when she reached up and smoothed her hair. "I know I don't look so hot in the mornings. Autumn always looks beautiful when she wakes up. I look like I just crawled out of a hole."

Her insecurity with her sisters broke his heart.

She had nothing to be insecure about. She was perfect. Just like that, he got the answer to his question. Spring was perfect. She was perfect for him.

He'd been looking for a companion. Someone he could not only talk to, but also have great sex with. And he'd found her. He liked her body, but he also liked her brain and her personality and her caring nature. He trusted her to keep his professional life professional and his private life private. That's what made her different from all the other women. They had all been missing something. But Spring wasn't missing anything. She was the total package. His total package.

He pulled her into his arms and tucked her close to his heart. He rested his chin on her head and took a deep breath of the scent that was uniquely Spring. "You're perfect just the way you are. So go home and change and I'll save you a seat at church."

She pulled back. "But if we sit in church together, people will think we're a couple."

He brushed the blue-tipped strand of hair from her eyes. "I realize that things are moving a little quickly. And I don't want to push you into anything you're not comfortable with. But the thing is, after last night, I kind of feel like a couple."

Her eyes widened. "But what about the gossip?"

"People gossip all the time about one thing or another. It gives them something to do. I'm not too worried about it."

"But if it gets too bad, you could get fired."

"As long as someone doesn't catch us having sex on my desk, I think we're good. Although I don't know how I'm going to resist. The desk fantasy has been riding me hard ever since you brought it up." He grinned. "And maybe a little before you brought it up."

"I knew it!" She pointed a finger at him. "You wanted me, Sheriff Kendall."

He tightened his hands on her waist and kissed her finger. "Correction. I want you, Miss Hadley. Badly."

Her eyes filled with heat, and she smiled. "How badly?" She released the sheet, and it slipped to the floor.

They were both late getting to church. But the phenomenal shower sex was well worth the censorious look the pastor gave them when first Waylon slipped into the back pew, and then a few minutes later, Spring joined him. She had changed into a flirty pink dress that reminded him of spun cotton candy. And during the rest of the service, he couldn't stop thinking about taking a bite and letting Spring's sugary sweetness melt in his mouth.

When they stood for the last hymn, he covered her fingers with his as they shared a hymnal. He hadn't been to church since becoming the sheriff. He'd looked forward to having his Sunday mornings free of watching out for the townsfolk. But as he stood next to Spring singing, he glanced up at the wooden cross over the pulpit and had an epiphany.

He couldn't keep every citizen in town safe every second of every day. No matter how good of a sheriff you were that was an impossibility. All he could do was his job and try to keep the townsfolk safe to the best of his ability. The rest he needed to leave to a higher power.

As the congregation was dismissed, no one

seemed to care that he and Spring were together. They greeted both of them with cheerful smiles and comments on how well the dance went before they continued on their way down the aisle. The only one who stopped was Ms. Marble.

"It's been a while since you've come to church, Waylon James." She glanced at Spring. "Atoning for sins?"

Waylon felt his cheeks heat as he replied. "I'm sure I have plenty that I need to atone for."

Ms. Marble smiled. "Don't we all." She winked at Spring. "Now if you two will excuse me, I've got some baking to do."

Once she was gone, Spring released her breath. "I think she knows."

Waylon took her arm and led her out of the church, nodding a greeting to people as they passed. "If she does, she doesn't look too upset about it."

"Because she's thinking we're going to get married. She doesn't think we're just enjoying a . . . spring fling."

Waylon laughed. "Is that what we had last night?"

She glanced over at him as they walked out into the parking lot. "What word would you use?"

He only had to think for a moment before he found one. And not just one, but a thousand. "Amazing. Phenomenal. Mind-blowing. Awesome. Incredible." He smiled. "Should I go on?"

She flashed a bright smile. "It was all those things, wasn't it?"

He had never wanted to kiss a woman as badly as he wanted to kiss Spring at that moment. He wanted to pull her into his arms and cover those pretty lips with his, and he didn't care who saw him do it. But before he could reach for her, Tucker pulled up in his patrol car and rolled down his window.

"Hey, Sheriff. I've been looking all over for you. Did your phone die?"

"No. I left it at home." He winked at Spring. "Someone told me that I needed to take a day off occasionally."

Tucker looked at Spring and blushed. "I hope you aren't mad at me for last night, Spring. I guess I was just feeling my oats. And I wanted to make it up to you by taking you to the Blake Shelton concert in Austin next month. I got me two tickets, front row and center—"

Waylon cut in. "Why were you looking for me, Tucker? Is there a problem?"

"We got us a 10-79, sheriff."

"A bomb threat?"

Tucker's eye turned confused. "No, I thought that was the code for vandalism. Anyway, some high school kids got a little full of themselves last night after the dance and painted some graffiti on the side of Tom Alford's barn. He said it looked just like a big—" He stopped and shot a glance over at Spring before he cleared his throat. "He caught the boys red-handed and identified them before they raced off. Do you want me to haul them in or do you want to do it?"

A month ago, he would've wanted to haul the boys in himself so he could read them the riot act before turning them over to the juvenile courts. But that was when he was still trying to act like a big bad sheriff. When he was still trying to fill his daddy's shoes. But truth was that his dad never would've hauled in young kids for just letting off some steam. He would've found a more appropriate way to teach them a lesson.

"I don't think hauling them in will be necessary," he said. "Let them sweat it out for a day, and then I'll stop by their houses tomorrow and have a little chat with them and their parents."

"But Tom's madder than a hornet. He wants to press charges."

"Why don't you call Tom and see if he'll change his mind if his barn gets sanded and painted for free? That should keep those boys out of trouble for a while."

Tucker grinned. "Yes sir, Sheriff. I'll let you know what he says."

"Not today. Call me tomorrow. Like I said before, I'm taking today off. I trust you and Jonas can handle things."

Tucker saluted. "Yes sir."

When he was gone, Spring smiled at him. "It's about time you took a day off. Are you going fishing?"

He winked. "Yep. And I hope I catch what I'm fishing for."

She caught onto his double entendre immediately. "Oh, no. I'm not going to let you spend your only day off in bed. Especially on a beautiful spring day like this." She hooked her arm through his and pulled him toward his truck. "We're going on a picnic."

They picked up sandwiches, potato salad, and some of Ms. Marble's oatmeal raisin cookies from Lucy's Place Diner and headed out of town. It *was* a beautiful day. The sun was shining. The bluebonnets were blooming. And Spring was here . . . sitting right next to him.

He planned on taking her to Whispering Falls. As a kid, he had gone swimming there with Raff, Zane, and Cole. It was a pretty spot on Arrington land with lots of shade trees and a clear creek that cascaded over a rocky ledge in an impressive waterfall. This early, the water would be too cold to swim in, but it was a perfect place for a picnic. And maybe a little snuggling.

But when he came to the fork in the road, instead of taking the left turn that led to Whispering Falls, he took the right turn.

Spring immediately sat up. "Where are we going?" Before he could answer, they passed the land where Spring's vintage trailer was parked. Or used to be parked. It was no longer there.

"Where's your trailer?" he asked. When she didn't answer right away, he glanced over to see her staring out the window at the vacant lot.

"Umm . . . I moved it."

"Where? I thought your Jeep was broken."

"It is. I had Dirk move it closer to his house. You were right. I was scared being all the way out here by myself." She sent him a bright smile. "So where are we going on our picnic?"

Waylon winked. "It's a surprise."

Although it wasn't much of a surprise. As soon as they pulled up to the corpse of trees, Spring knew where they were. "The little white chapel!" She jumped out and headed down the path that led through the trees. He got a blanket from the back and their bags of food, then hurried to catch up with her.

"I figured you'd like my choice," he said as he took her hand. "All women seem to love the little white chapel."

"Because it's the place where dreams come true."

He chuckled. "You make it sound like the baseball field in the movie *Field of Dreams.*"

"For women, it's just like that. It's the place where all the mail-order brides were married—the real ones and the fictional ones that Lucy Arrington wrote about in her Tender Heart series. A place filled with happily-ever-afters." She tugged him into the clearing and released a gasp. "Oh my gosh. I've never seen it in the spring. It's beautiful."

Waylon had to agree. The little white chapel had always been pretty with its pristine white siding, tall stately spire, and stained-glass windows. But in spring, it was breathtaking. The open field that surrounded the church was filled with vibrant bluish-purple bluebonnets. And maybe it wasn't spring that made it breathtaking as much as Spring.

She tugged him through the field of flowers, her dark hair and pretty pink dress fluttering in the breeze. She stopped right in front of the chapel and lifted her gaze to the tall spire, then closed her eyes.

He didn't need to ask what she was doing. All the girls in high school had whispered about the legend of the chapel. A legend that said if you made a wish on the chapel's spire for true love, you'd find it.

Waylon had always thought the legend was silly. But as he looked at Spring's beautiful profile turned toward the clear blue sky, it didn't seem silly at all. In fact, suddenly, he believed in magic. Suddenly, he believed that dreams could come true.

With Spring's hand tucked securely in his, he turned toward the church, closed his eyes, and made a wish.

CHAPTER NINETEEN

SPRING WASN'T JUST HAPPY. SHE was down-right giddy. She tried to blame the giddiness on sexual satisfaction. Waylon was an amazing lover. He was attentive, thorough, patient, and had figured out all her hot spots. He knew where to kiss her neck to make her tremble. How to caress her breasts to make her knees weak. And what angle to thrust to send her over the moon. Any woman would be giddy with sexual satisfaction after spending two weeks in Waylon's bed.

Every night, she parked in his garage and snuck into his house. Dirk thought she was staying in her trailer, but Spring thought Gracie knew better. There was a sparkle in her sister-in-law's eyes whenever Spring made excuses for why she couldn't come to dinner or stop by the house.

Spring wanted to talk to Gracie. Maybe she could shed some light on the giddy feeling. But she worried that if the news of her affair with Waylon got out it would damage his reputation. He might act like he didn't care, but deep down she knew that he did. He wasn't as straight-laced as he used to be, but he still wanted to make his father and the townsfolk proud of him. Plus, she didn't want him to lose his job. He loved being a sheriff. And the more he relaxed, the better sheriff he became.

Although he still had his moments.

"Miss Hadley!"

She smiled as she got up and headed to his office. He sat behind his desk staring at the new screensaver she'd put on that morning when he was out on patrol. "Yes, Sheriff Kendall?" she asked innocently.

He swiveled his chair and pointed to the screen. "What's that?"

She bit back a smile. "It's a shirtless cowboy straddling a fence. I thought you said you wanted something more masculine."

His lips twitched. "That's not what I had in mind."

"Sorry, sir. Would you like the dancing pugs back?"

"As a matter of fact, I would. Those pugs were pretty cute. In fact, I've been thinking about getting one. Sherlock could use a buddy."

"I think that's a great idea," she said. "Is there anything else, sir?"

He got up and moved around his desk. "There are a couple things I want to discuss. Did you get on my personal laptop and cancel my subscription to the online dating site?"

She held his gaze. "Yes."

His lips twitched again. "Good. I've been wanting to do it, but I've been extremely busy—what with my new demanding girlfriend."

"Demanding?"

He leaned on the desk and crossed his arms. "The woman can't seem to get enough. But I shouldn't be talking about that with my assistant. Totally improper."

"Totally." She lifted an eyebrow. "Is that all you needed, Sheriff?"

"No. I need something else. Unfortunately, that would also be improper." He glanced down at his desk. "But I think about it . . . a lot. And one day, I don't think I'm going to be able to stop myself."

Talk about melting panties. Spring's incinerated. She released a breathy moan that made Waylon's eyes heat.

He glanced at the clock on the wall. "Two hours and twenty-two minutes before we can go home. I'll warn you now, Miss Hadley. You aren't going to make it past the foyer."

Her grip tightened on the doorknob, and her voice hit a high note when she spoke. "I'll look forward to it, sir." She pulled the door closed behind her, then stood there for a moment with her forehead pressed against the lacquered wood. The front door opened, and she collected her tingling female parts and turned to find her two sisters standing just inside the door.

She had missed them, but she didn't realize how much until this moment. She didn't hesitate to walk straight over and pull them into her arms. They didn't say anything. They didn't have to. Their communication had always run deeper than words. They stood with their arms linked and their dark heads touching. Spring felt like two of her body parts had reattached. She'd been happy before, but now she felt complete. Autumn and

Summer must've felt the same way. When they lifted their heads, their eyes locked and identical smiles lit their faces.

Then Summer had to ruin the connection by stepping back and opening her mouth. "Okay, office playtime is over. It's time to get your butt back to the real world."

Autumn glared at her. "I told you to let me do the talking."

"I know what you told me, but I've never been good at taking orders. And you've never been good at communicating. You'd be happy to spend the rest of your life in a tower filled with books and never talk to a single soul ever again."

Autumn heaved a sigh and crossed her arms. "Say you're sorry."

Summer turned to Spring. Her eyes were sincere. "I'm sorry. I shouldn't have lost my temper."

"And?" Autumn prodded.

"And you're not a ditz. Now go pack your stuff and let's go home." Summer paused. "Please."

This is what Spring had wanted. She'd wanted Summer to apologize and beg her to come back home. Suddenly, she realized how childish and irresponsible her behavior had been. She owned a portion of the business. If she wanted an apology, she should've stayed in Houston and stood up to her sister and demanded one. Instead, she'd run off like the spoiled youngest triplet she was. No wonder Summer thought she was a ditz. She'd acted like one. An immature, irresponsible ditz. And her time away from her sisters had helped her to see that. Granny had been right. As much as she missed her sisters, she'd needed time away from them to find herself. To grow up.

"I'm sorry too," she said.

"You don't need to apologize, Spring," Autumn said. "Summer and I both know you didn't mean to leave the back door unlocked."

Spring shook her head. "I'm not apologizing for leaving the door open. That was an accident. I'm apologizing for running off without a word. That was irresponsible and immature."

"You're damn straight it was," Summer said. "Now let's go."

"I'm not leaving."

Summer scowled. "Stop being a—"

Autumn cut her off. "She's right. She can't just walk out on her job. She'll need to give the sheriff at least a week's notice so he can find someone else."

"I'm not giving him notice," she said. "I took this job and I'm staying until Gail comes back. I couldn't leave Waylon without an assistant."

Summer released an exasperated huff. "You're just being hardheaded, Spring. I'm sure you're not that indispensable to the sheriff."

"Stop it, Summer," Autumn said. "I think it's admirable that Spring wants to stay until the sheriff's assistant gets back."

"But we need her at the store. We can't lose any more customers."

"Sales are still down?" Spring asked.

"Way down," Autumn replied. "If they don't come up by the end of this quarter, we'll have to close."

Spring was ready to let the store go. It had never been her dream. And she wasn't so sure it was

Autumn's either. They both had been bulldozed by Summer. But Spring couldn't let herself be bulldozed any more.

"I'm sorry that the store isn't doing well, but I'm not going back to Houston."

"What do you mean you're not coming back?" Summer said.

Her answer came easily. "I mean I don't want to live in Houston. I want to live here in Bliss."

Summer stared at her for only a second before she turned at Autumn. "I told you something was going on with her and the sheriff. All he did at lunch was sing her praises about what an honest, dependable, hardworking woman she was." She looked back at Spring. "Please don't tell me you're in love."

Spring started to deny it, but before the denial could get past her throat, the truth dawned. She wasn't giddy because she was sexually satisfied. She was giddy because she *was* in love. In love with Sheriff Waylon Kendall.

Autumn eyes widened as she watched Spring. "I was trying to put my finger on what's different about you. But that's it, isn't it? You've fallen in love."

Before Spring could reply, the front door opened and Mrs. Miller stepped in. She was carrying a little gray kitten in the crook of her arm. She glanced at Spring's sisters.

"Goodness gracious, you three are as identical as your nieces. Although I've watched the babies enough to be able to tell them apart." She looked at Spring and smiled. "Which is why I'm here. Dirk and Gracie spread the word about what a good job

I've done watching the triplets, and this Granny Nanny is booked until after Memorial Day with babysitting jobs."

"Oh my gosh!" Spring gave Mrs. Miller a hug, careful not to squash the cute little kitten. "That's wonderful news."

"I have you to thank for it."

"I didn't do anything, Mrs. Miller. All I did was make a suggestion to Gracie. She's thrilled to have the help."

Tears came into Mrs. Miller's eyes. "You did much more than that, young lady. You gave a lonely woman something to worry about besides her cats. You gave me a new lease on life." She held out the kitten. "And I wanted you to have the pick of Mirabelle's litter. Of course, she won't be ready to leave her mama for another couple weeks."

"Aww," she took the kitten and cuddled it close. "Aren't you the cutest little thing ever?" While Spring was making a fuss over the cat, Jonas came in.

"There's a no animals rule in the office," he said. A grin spread over his face. "But I guess I can let it slide this time."

Spring glanced at the clock. "You're early for your shift. Is something wrong?"

His smile got bigger. "Actually, everything's right. I came to work early because I wanted to tell you that I've decided to retire and move to Fort Worth where my son and his family live." He stood a little taller. "I got a job teaching classes at the sheriff's training academy there. It's just part time, but I figure between it and my grandkids I should be kept pretty busy."

"I'm so happy for you." Jonas had made it perfectly clear that he wasn't a hugger, but she couldn't help giving him one.

He even gave her a little squeeze back before he cleared his throat. "Well, I better go take a nap so I'll be ready for the nightshift." He tipped his hat at her sisters and Mrs. Miller, who blushed the prettiest shade of pink.

Spring was struck by what a cute couple they made. But before she could do a little matchmaking, the phone rang. For the next fifteen minutes, she had to deal with a flood of phone calls about the traffic light on Main Street being broken. In between calls, she radioed Tucker and sent him to direct traffic. Then she called Doug Hansen, who had fixed the troublesome light before. When she had finally finished dealing with the light problem, she turned to her sisters who had taken seats in the reception area. They were both staring at her as if they didn't recognize her.

"What?" she asked.

Autumn smiled. "Granny Bon was right."

"That's why we didn't come to Bliss sooner," Summer said. "Granny Bon made us promise to stop suffocating you. She was convinced you needed time away from us so you could grow up." Granny Bon was the only person Summer listened to. Or sort of listened to.

"So that's why you tried to get Waylon to talk me into coming home," Spring said. "That way you could keep your promise to Granny, but still get me to come back."

"It didn't work. Waylon refused to help me." Summer studied her. "And now I know why.

Not only is he daffy in love with you, but you're damned good at your job."

The unexpected praise brought tears to Spring's eyes. Or maybe it was the combination of her sister's praise and the thought of Waylon loving her. She wished with all her heart that it was true. But he hadn't said a word about love. And maybe he was just waiting for her to say the words first.

"Come on, Summer." Autumn got to her feet. "Let's let Spring get back to work and go see our nieces."

Summer stood and studied Spring. "You're really not coming back?"

More tears filled her eyes as she shook her head. "I'm happy here, Summer."

Summer nodded before she pulled Spring in for a tight, bone-crushing hug. "I love you, Spring Leigh Hadley. I might've been harder on you than Dirk or Autumn, but that's only because I didn't think you were living up to your potential. You are an amazing woman. I'm sorry if I kept you from finding that out sooner."

Tears dripped down Spring's face. "Oh, Summer. I'm going to miss you and Autumn so much."

Autumn placed her arms around her sisters and joined the hug. "No one is going to miss anyone. It's not like we live in Timbuktu. Houston is only a couple hours away. Now that we don't have to worry about our promise to Granny Bon, we can visit all we want."

Summer pulled back. "She's right. We'll see each other a lot. In fact, this summer, let's take a camping trip together in your little ham can."

"That's if Daddy ever brings it back." The words

just popped out, but Spring was glad they did. She was tired of hiding the truth.

Summer's eyes narrowed. "Don't tell me you loaned Daddy your camper, Spring."

"Not loaned exactly. He took it without my permission, but he promised to bring it and my Jeep back."

Summer groaned and shook her head. "You might've become responsible, but you're still gullible. Daddy isn't going to bring them back. Especially when he's running from the law."

CHAPTER TWENTY

"YOU PROBABLY USED A BAD picture," Waylon's mother said. "That's the only explanation for why online dating didn't work for you. You're a handsome, intelligent man with a great job and beautiful home. What woman wouldn't want to date you?"

Waylon smiled and adjusted the phone to his ear. "Thanks, Mom."

"You're welcome, but don't be getting a big head. You're also stubborn and single-minded like your father. But hopefully the women won't figure that out until after you hook them with your charm. When you come for Easter I'll have your father take another photograph of you. He's become quite good at photography now that he's retired."

Waylon was surprised. When he was growing up, his dad hadn't known one end of a camera from the other. "I don't need Dad to take another picture, Mom. I no longer belong to the online dating site."

"But you didn't even give it a good college try before you quit."

"I tried it, Mom. And it might work for some people, but it didn't work for me." He could feel her disappointment seeping through the receiver. Since he never liked to disappoint his mother, he got to the reason he'd called her in the first place. "There's someone I'm bringing with me when I come for Easter."

"Did you get another dog? I've always thought that Sherlock needed a friend to perk him up. That has to be the laziest dog I've ever seen in my life."

"He's not lazy. He just enjoys sleeping better than exercising. And I'm not talking about a dog."

"Is it your new deputy, Tucker? I've been looking forward to meeting him. He sounds like a nice young man. Even if he is a little overzealous. You were overzealous too when you first started—"

He cut in because his mother could ramble on forever. Just like someone else he knew. "It's a woman."

There was a long stretch of silence before his mother released a squeal that almost broke his eardrum. "Thank the Lord! My prayers have been answered. Who is she? Does she live in Bliss? Please don't tell me it's Winnie Crawley? No, I take that back. If she makes you happy, I don't care if it's Winnie."

"It's not Winnie. You've never met her, but you've talked to her on the phone."

"Your new assistant? I was hoping you'd fall head over heels in love with that sweet little gal."

He started to correct his mother, but then realized that she was right. He *had* fallen head over heels in love with Spring. He'd known it for a long time. He just hadn't put it into words. It was surprising how good it felt when he did.

"I do love her, Mom."

"Oh, Waylon," his mother's voice held joy and tears. "I'm so happy for you, son. And if you love her, I know I'll love her too. I'm halfway there already after talking to her on the phone. Now give me all the details."

He had never been good at giving his mother details about his other girlfriends, but he found he had no problem talking about Spring. By the time he ended the conversation, his mother probably thought he was a lovesick fool. But he didn't care. He wanted to tell everyone about his feelings for Spring. He wanted to walk down the street with her on his arm and let the whole world know that she was his girl.

But first he needed to tell Spring.

He wanted to do it right. Red roses. A romantic dinner in Austin. While he was looking up florists on his computer, Luke called. And since the kid only texted him when he wanted to practice baseball, Waylon got a little concerned.

"What's up, Luke? Everything okay at home?"

"Yeah. I mean Raff is driving Savannah crazy with his overprotectiveness, but other than that, things are good."

"Did you want to meet this afternoon?" Luke didn't need any more instruction. The last few games he'd played great, and the team had a good chance of going to the state playoffs. And maybe that's why Luke had called. He was feeling nervous and just needed some reassurance. "Although you don't really need my help anymore. You've been doing an amazing job in center field. And that double you hit was crucial to winning the last game."

"Thanks," Luke said. There was another long pause before he added. "Actually, I'm calling to tell you thanks for coaching me. I know I wasn't exactly cool about it to begin with. And I just wanted you to know I appreciate the help."

Waylon smiled. "You're welcome. I enjoyed it as much as you did. If you ever want to toss the ball around after school, you let me know."

"I can't. I've started doing homework after school with Cheryl Gibbs."

Waylon's smile got bigger. "Yep, you don't want those grades to slide. And Cheryl Gibbs seems like a smart young lady . . . pretty too." There was a tap on his door, and Spring peeked her head in.

"Oh, I'm sorry," she said. "I didn't realize you were on the phone."

Talk about pretty girls. Just the sight of Spring made Waylon's heart beat faster. And suddenly, he realized he couldn't wait until dinner to let her know how he felt. "Thanks for calling, Luke. But I better get back to work."

Once he'd hung up, he stood and came around his desk. "Is there something you needed, Miss Hadley?" There was something he needed. Her. In his arms. Forever. But before he could bring that up, he noticed her pale face and serious expression. He was instantly concerned. "What's wrong? Did you have a relapse of the flu?"

She shook her head. "I just need to talk to you."

His shouldered relaxed. "That's funny because I need to talk to you too. But ladies first."

She fidgeted with the skirt of her dress. "Remember when you came out to the—" The sound of the front door opening had her cutting off and glancing behind her. "Could I help you?"

Sheriff Dan Wainwright appeared. He was an older sheriff from the next county who was close friends with Waylon's father. Waylon immediately walked over to shake his hand and greet him. "Hey, Dan. It's good to see you. This is my new assistant, Spring Hadley. Spring, this is Sheriff Dan Wainwright."

Dan had always been a jolly sheriff, much more easygoing than Waylon's father. But he seemed almost hesitant when he took off his hat and nodded at Spring. "Ma'am." He looked at Waylon. "Could I speak with you in private, Way?"

Obviously, he was there on serious business. Waylon nodded. "Of course. If you'll excuse us, Miss Hadley."

"It was nice to meet you, Sheriff Wainwright," she said before she stepped out the door and closed it behind her.

When she was gone, Waylon walked around his desk and sat down. "What's going on, Dan?"

Dan sat down in the chair and hooked his hat on his knee. His eyes widened when he glanced at the computer screen that was still turned at an angle. Waylon remembered the half-naked cowboy screensaver and quickly turned the monitor. But it was too late. If his confused expression was any indication, Dan had already seen it.

"It was just a joke," Waylon said lamely.

Dan seemed at a loss for words. "That's . . . real funny." Since more excuses would only make things worse, Waylon kept his mouth shut and waited for

Dan to explain why he was there. It didn't take him long. "Did Holt Hadley ever show up here?"

Waylon shook his head. "No. I would've called Mike if he had."

Dan nodded. "I figured as much." He tapped his hat on his knee. "They found him. Like most everyone had figured, Holt was headed for the border. New Mexico state patrol picked him up outside of Las Cruces."

Damn. He wished Dan had waited a day to give him the information. Now he'd have to tell Spring. And that certainly threw a wet blanket on his plans to tell her that he loved her. He had little doubt that Spring would be upset about her father's arrest.

"Thanks for stopping by to let me know, Dan."

Dan continued to tap his hat. "That's not the reason I stopped by. Holt got so far because he had ditched his car and was driving another vehicle."

"He stole a car?"

"We don't think he stole it. We think it was given to him."

Waylon rested his hands on the desk. "Are you thinking that Dirk gave him a car and then lied about it? He's not that kind of man. Besides, Dirk and his wife Gracie only have four vehicles, and I've seen all of them in town in the last week."

Dan studied Waylon. "I don't think it was his son who gave Holt a vehicle. It was his daughter."

Waylon was surprised. "Autumn or Summer?"

He glanced at the closed door. "Neither."

When the truth dawned on him, Waylon shook his head. "You're way off track on this one, Dan. Spring has been here in Bliss for the last two months. She hasn't seen her father. If she had, she would've told me."

Dan held Waylon's gaze. "The white Jeep Holt was driving was registered to Spring Leigh Hadley."

Waylon felt his insides tighten. "Then he must've stolen it."

"Spring's Jeep was reported stolen?"

Waylon suddenly felt like he had when he'd gotten the flu—off-balance and unable to put his thoughts in any kind of coherent order. Or maybe he just refused to see the picture all the pieces had fallen into. Spring hadn't said a word about her Jeep being stolen. She had claimed it had broken down. Which was why she was driving Dirk's old ranch truck. But if her Jeep was broken why wasn't it at Emmett's garage?

"Holt was also found with a trailer," Dan said. "One of those tiny vintage ones. Pink with Spring Fling written across the back." When Waylon only stared at him, he released his breath in a long sigh. "Damn, Way. I thought you weren't the type of man to get sucked in by a pair of pretty blue eyes." He shook his head. "I thought your daddy taught you better."

His father had taught him better. But Waylon was obviously a slow learner. Even now he couldn't quite believe it. But the proof was in the pudding, as his mother always said. And everything pointed to Spring helping her fugitive father to escape the country . . . and then lying to Waylon about it.

He glanced at the office door. "Are you here to arrest her?"

Dan studied him. "No. I'm here because your daddy is my friend. And I don't want this coming back to bite you in the ass. You should know that as sheriff, you're constantly under a microscope. You can't move without people talking. And the talk is that you and your assistant have started playing house. Now that would be okay if she was a sweet hometown girl who didn't break the law. But Spring abetted a fugitive. And if you don't want shit on your face, you need to fire her before the feds get here to question her." He got up and put his hat on. "And we never had this conversation." He turned and walked out.

When he was gone, Waylon fell back in his chair and ran a hand through this hair. There had to be a mistake. The Spring he knew wasn't a criminal or a liar. She *was* sweet and kind and honest.

"Waylon?"

The softly spoken word made his insides tighten. He looked up and saw Spring standing in the doorway.

"Where are your Jeep and trailer, Spring?"

Her face grew even paler, and the guilt in her eyes was easy to read. Still, he couldn't accept the truth. Because if he accepted it, everything she'd made him believe in would be nothing but a lie. And he couldn't deal with that. He damn well couldn't deal with it. So he just sat there and didn't say anything. He didn't ask for an explanation or the truth because he didn't want either. He wanted things to stay the same.

But then Spring spoke, and everything changed. "My father has them."

He wanted to cover his ears and shout at her to shut up. Instead he sat there while the woman he thought he knew turned into someone he didn't know at all.

"But you have to believe me, Waylon," she continued in a pleading voice. "I didn't know he was running from the law. When he showed up, he acted like he just wanted to go camping with me. And I should've known something was wrong when he hid in the bathroom the night you came to my trailer."

He stared at her. "He was there that night I came to the trailer? The night I smelled the cigarette smoke?"

"Yes."

He finally woke up from the trance he'd been in. "You lied. You lied about it all. The cigarette smoke. Your trailer. Your Jeep."

She moved closer to the desk. "But only because I didn't want Dirk to find out my daddy was there and start a family squabble. I didn't keep the secret from you to hide my father from the law. I swear I would never put your job in jeopardy like that. I just fell for my daddy's lie. I'm just a stupid, gullible ditz."

He shook head. "I don't believe you. Because the woman who's worked for me the last few weeks is far from gullible. She's intelligent, capable, and intuitive enough to know a lie when she sees one. If hiding in your bathroom when I showed up wasn't a big enough clue that he was on the lam, stealing your Jeep and trailer should've been. But he didn't steal it, did he, Spring? You gave them both to him, and then you straight faced lied to me about it."

Her eyes widened. "How can you say that?"

His gaze locked with hers. "How can I not?"

Tears welled and trickled down her cheeks, but he refused to fall for that ploy again. "I thought you knew me," she whispered. "I thought you knew me better than anyone. But you don't know me at all."

He turned his back to her and stared at the sheriff's creed on the wall. "You're right. I don't know you. And I don't want to know you. You're fired, Miss Hadley. I want you gone today. Right now."

He waited for her to say something. Waited for her to plead her case. And maybe he wasn't waiting as much as praying. Praying that she'd say something that would make everything right. But she didn't. After the clock had ticked through a full minute, he finally glanced over his shoulder.

Spring was gone.

And all that was left was a harsh, cold winter.

CHAPTER TWENTY-ONE

GRANNY BON'S HOUSE HAD CHANGED very little since Spring had lived there. The front path was still buckled from the roots of the big oak tree that she and her siblings had climbed. The porch swing still squeaked loudly enough to alert Granny of any overzealous teenage boys attempting to kiss her granddaughters. And inside, the walls still held the scent of Granny's favorite lavender air freshener . . . and love.

Spring had thought that returning to Granny Bon's house in Waco would make her feel better, but it didn't. Not even her sisters snuggled on either side of her made her feel better. When she'd left Houston, she'd felt like two of her limbs were missing. But now she felt like her entire heart was missing. There was a huge hole in her chest that couldn't be filled by her sisters. Only one person could fill it. And that person was never going to talk to her again.

Tears filled her eyes and slid down her cheeks as she stared at the ceiling above the bed. There was old tape on the popcorn plaster from all the posters of boy band idols Spring had taped up, a few spidery cracks from where Summer had misjudged her softball tosses, and one faded photograph of their mama that Autumn had tacked up.

The triplets looked just like Dotty Hadley. Same jet-black hair. Same deep blue eyes. Same full lips. But her mother's personality traits had been divided between the three of them. Summer had gotten her determination and tenacity. Autumn had gotten her love of books and calm disposition. And Spring had gotten her weakness for believing Holt Hadley's lies.

How could she have been so stupid? How could she believe that her father just wanted to go on a fishing trip to Mexico? He probably hadn't fished a day in his life. And why hadn't she been more suspicious when he'd gotten so freaked out when Waylon showed up? She should've known something was wrong when Holt had hidden in the bathroom. It was true that Dirk would've been upset if he'd found out Holt had been there, but her father had never cared about upsetting Dirk before. Or keeping peace in the family. Spring was the only one who worried about that. And if she hadn't been so determined to bring her family back together, she wouldn't be lying there with a hole in her chest. She'd be back in Bliss making Waylon his morning coffee.

She'd really screwed up this time. It was one thing to leave a door unlocked and another to straight-faced lie to a sheriff. Especially when you loved that sheriff with all your heart. Waylon had trusted her, and she'd betrayed that trust. She'd seen the hurt from that betrayal in his eyes. And she hadn't just hurt him emotionally. She'd hurt him professionally. Before she left, the town was abuzz with gossip about how the sheriff had been bamboozled by Holt Hadley and his daughter. All Waylon had wanted was for the townsfolk to respect him, and Spring had taken all their respect and flushed it right down the toilet.

A double rap on the door drew her attention away from her thoughts. She knew the rap. She'd heard it hundreds of times before. She also knew it would be followed by her Granny Bon peeking her head in. Not wanting to talk to her grandmother, she closed her eyes and pretended to sleep. She should've known better. Nothing got past Granny Bon.

A second after the door creaked open, Granny Bon spoke. "I know you're awake, Spring Leigh. You never were good at pretense."

Spring opened her eyes to see her grandmother standing at the foot of the bed. She was dressed for work in her polyester black pants and floral top. Her salt and pepper hair pulled back in a braid. She had never worn makeup, and her face held very few wrinkles. Of course, both she and her daughter had been teen mothers so she was young for a woman with adult grandkids.

"Breakfast is ready," she said in her no-nonsense voice. "Don't wake your sisters. I want to talk to you alone." Then she swept out of the room without giving Spring a chance to decline. Not that it would've done any good. When Granny gave an order, you followed it. And there was little doubt that her grandmother had ordered her to breakfast.

Since there was no way out of it, she carefully

untangled herself from her sisters. Summer was hardest to get away from. For being such a hard-ass, she was the biggest cuddler. She grumbled in her sleep as Spring slipped beneath her arm, then snuggled closer to Autumn and went back to sleep.

When Spring got to the breakfast table, Granny Bon was sitting and reading the morning newspaper as if she had no desire to talk. Two places were set with Granny's usual breakfast—a bowl of steel-cut oats with blueberries, a slice of whole-wheat toast with no butter, and a glass of orange juice with no pulp. Granny's orange juice was in a juice glass. Spring's was in a Disney princess glass. One of the same Disney princess glasses Holt had given her and her sisters on their sixth birthday. It was the only birthday gift they'd ever received from him. Just the sight of it made Spring want to swipe it off the table and send it crashing to the floor.

"I won't drink out of that glass," she said between clenched teeth.

Granny Bon's gray eyes peeked over the edge of the newspaper. "Sorry, but the other glasses are dirty. And sometimes we just have to drink out of the glasses we're given."

There was a lesson in there somewhere. There was always a lesson with Granny Bon. But Spring was too upset to figure it out. "I hate him." She flopped down in the chair. "I really, really hate him."

Granny Bon carefully folded the newspaper and tucked it under the plastic napkin holder in the center of the table. "No, you don't. You love him. Which is where all your anger comes from. We want the people we love to be perfect. But that's just not how life works. Your daddy isn't perfect. In fact, he's about as imperfect as a man can get. That doesn't mean you get to hate him. Hate is worse for the hater than it is for the person being hated."

Spring didn't even try to blink back her tears. "But how could he do it? I thought he'd turned over a new leaf. I thought he was trying to change. But he hasn't changed at all. He's still the worst father in all of Texas. No, in the entire world. He never loved Mama and he certainly doesn't love us kids. Did you realize because of him I was investigated by the FBI? If I hadn't been able to convince them that I didn't know Daddy was a fugitive, I might've gone to jail."

"I can't argue that Holt has always been a poor excuse for a husband and father, but I won't sit here and let you blame him for your own mistakes." Granny Bon sent her a stern look. "Holt didn't hold a gun to your head and force you to lie. If you'd reported him as soon as you discovered your Jeep and trailer missing, you wouldn't have been in trouble with the FBI."

Spring's butt came up off the chair. "But you just said I had to love my daddy! How do you love your daddy and turn him in to the police?"

"I said you shouldn't hate him. I did not say you had to put up with his shenanigans. You should know by now that your father is manipulative and untrustworthy. And I don't think that's ever gonna change. So love him, but don't condone his behavior. That's what your mama did, and she had nothing but heartache because of it. She just couldn't see people's faults. And that can be a good thing, but it also can be a very bad one."

Spring wiped the tears from her cheeks. "This time, it's a very bad one. I hurt someone, Granny Bon. I hurt someone that didn't deserve to be hurt. I'm no better than Daddy."

Granny Bon pulled a paper napkin out of the holder and handed it to her. "You're nothing like your daddy, Spring Leigh. He only cares about himself and you care about everyone but yourself. Ever since you were a child, you tried to make people happy. You'd make funny faces to get Dirk to laugh, take responsibility for something you didn't do so Summer wouldn't get a spanking, and meet me at the door when I got home from work with a cold glass of iced tea and a bright smile." She reached out and patted Spring's cheek. "You have a rare gift. All you have to do is smile to brighten someone's day. Which is why I'm having a hard time believing that you intentionally hurt someone."

"I didn't hurt Waylon intentionally. I just didn't want my siblings finding out that Daddy had stolen my car and trailer and getting mad at him."

"Are you sure you just didn't want them finding out that you'd been so gullible?"

Spring blew out her breath. "That too. After leaving the door of Seasons unlocked, I didn't want them to know that I'd made another stupid mistake." Her shoulders slumped. "A stupid mistake that has cost me the only man I've ever loved."

Granny Bon studied her. "And does the sheriff love you?"

"Not anymore. How could he possibly love me after what I did?" When Granny Bon picked up her spoon and started eating her oatmeal, Spring's eyes widened. "Well, aren't you going to tell me that I'm wrong? Aren't you going to tell me that if he loved me at all he wouldn't let a little mistake ruin everything? Because if you truly love someone, you forgive them. Aren't you going to tell me that?"

Her grandmother looked at her and lifted an eyebrow. "Obviously, I don't need to tell you. You already know."

Spring sighed. "So Waylon doesn't love me. And never truly did. Because if he loved me, he would've believed me when I told him that I didn't know about my daddy running from the law and he would've understood why I didn't tell him the truth."

"You really need to get a clue, Spring." Summer wandered into the room. Her hair was wild and her eyes squinty from the sun that poured in through the window of the breakfast nook. "Jesus, Granny, could you pull a shade? And please tell me you made coffee."

"It's in the pot," Granny Bon said. "But a young woman who uses the Lord's name in vain will not be getting a cup until she apologizes."

"To you or Jesus?" Granny Bon's eyebrow lifted, and Summer quickly acquiesced. "Fine, I'm sorry, Granny." She looked at the ceiling. "And Lord Jesus."

"Apologize to your sister for your hateful words."

Summer walked into the kitchen, opened a cupboard, and got out a mug. "I will not apologize for the truth. Just because Waylon got mad and fired her doesn't mean that he doesn't love her."

Just the thought of Waylon loving her had Spring

straightening. "What makes you say that?"

Summer poured herself some coffee. "Because Waylon sang your praises when we had lunch at the truck stop."

"Why did you have lunch at a truck stop with the sheriff, Summer Lynn?" Granny Bon asked.

Summer's eyes widened for a fraction of a second before she hedged around the question. "It doesn't matter. The point that I'm trying to make is that just because the sheriff got a little ticked doesn't mean that he doesn't love you. When you forgot to lock the back door, I ranted and raved at you too. But after you left and I had a chance to cool off, I realized that you didn't intentionally leave the door unlocked. You just got wrapped up helping Charlie and forgot."

"Charlie?" Spring stared at her sister. "You know the street guy's name?"

Summer took a sip of coffee. "Why do you think he was living in our alley? I made the mistake of buying him sandwiches whenever I got us lunch at the deli, and he followed me back to the store one day and camped out. Between me giving him food, you giving him clothes, and Autumn getting him set up at the homeless shelter, he found the right sisters to cling to."

Spring wasn't surprised her sister had never mentioned helping Charlie. Summer wasn't the type who liked people knowing she had a soft side. But she did. As a kid, she was always sticking up for the underdog at school or bringing home stray animals. Which was something Spring had forgotten during the stress of running the store.

"You're a good person, sis," she said.

Summer shrugged. "Only on occasion. But that's what I'm trying to get across to you. Sometimes, people say things they don't mean."

"So you think Waylon regrets the hateful things he said to me?"

Summer took a few sips of coffee before she answered. "It's possible. Or not. This screw-up was much worse than your last one. He might hate your guts forever and never talk to you again."

"Summer," Granny Bon's voice held a stern warning.

"What? I'm just being honest."

"Being honest and being brutally honest are two different things."

Spring turned to her grandmother. "What do you think, Granny Bon? Do you think there's a chance that Waylon might forgive me?"

"I think there's a very good chance, but the only way to find out is to go back to Bliss."

Just the thought of going back to Bliss and facing Waylon and the people of the town was terrifying. Especially when she had run off like a whipped pup with her tail between her legs. She had thought she was so grown up, but she certainly hadn't acted that way. A mature adult would've stayed and faced the music. Instead, once she'd been cleared by the FBI, she'd run from her problems just like she'd done when she left Houston. Obviously, she *was* a slow learner.

"Good morning." Autumn walked in. Unlike Spring and Summer, who still wore their pajamas, Autumn was showered and fully dressed without a hair out of place. She sent Spring a concerned look. "How are you feeling?"

Surprisingly, Spring realized that she felt better. Not good, but better. At least now there was a glimmer of hope. "I'm headed back to Bliss," she said. "I never should've left in the first place."

"That's my girl," Granny Bon patted her back.

But before Spring could get to her feet, Autumn stopped her. "I don't know if that's a good idea." Her eyes held concern and pity. "I just talked to Dirk, and he said that the town council has called a meeting this afternoon. They're going to decide whether or not to fire Waylon for conduct unbecoming a sheriff."

CHAPTER TWENTY-TWO

WAYLON GOT OUT OF BED at six o'clock. He showered and shaved, then dressed in a white t-shirt, pressed jeans, and the boots he'd polished in the wee hours of the morning to keep his mind from wandering places he didn't want it to go. He waited to put on his starched uniform shirt until after he'd eaten breakfast.

But once in the kitchen, he realized he wasn't hungry. When he started to make coffee and his mind wandered to the one place he didn't want it to go, he decided to skip the coffee as well as breakfast. He fed Sherlock, and then let the dog outside to do his business. The sun was just peeking over the horizon, tinting the skies a vibrant pink. The pink of frilly dresses. And pouting lips. And vintage trailers. The pink of Spring.

A pain seared through his chest, but he barely reacted to it. In the last few days, he had become immune to the pain. He waited for Sherlock to finish before he whistled. The dog took his time getting back to the house. Once inside, he flopped down on his bed by the stove and fell asleep.

Waylon wished he could join him. He was not looking forward to the day ahead. He wasn't looking forward to it at all. But he refused to take the cowardly way out. So he went upstairs to put on his shirt. Once he had it buttoned and tucked in tight, he picked up the sheriff's star on the dresser. Since this could be the last time he pinned on the star, he took his time. Once it was fastened above his pocket, he glanced at himself in the mirror. Even starched and polished, he looked like hell. The dark half-circles under his eyes spoke of his sleepless nights, and his eyes held a pain he could no longer ignore.

She'd left.

She'd left without a single word.

Her lies had punched him in the heart. Her leaving had ripped it out completely. Lying about her father proved she didn't trust him. Leaving proved she didn't care.

He studied his reflection in the mirror. At one time, he'd wondered if being a sheriff was what he really wanted or if he'd just gone along with it to please his father. But now that he feared he was about to lose his star, he realized how much he loved his job. He couldn't blame the city council for calling an emergency meeting. He should be held accountable for his actions. He'd been so wrapped up in Spring, he'd failed to protect the citizens of Bliss. If Holt had been a dangerous fugitive, innocent people could've been hurt.

But what would he do if he lost his job? He couldn't stay in Bliss. He couldn't live among people he'd so badly disappointed. He also couldn't stand there all day worrying about what might happen. He glanced once more at the star on his chest before he turned on a boot heel and walked out of the room.

He arrived at his office before seven. He expected the parking lot to be empty. But a familiar truck was parked next to the spot reserved for the sheriff. He parked in his spot and got out slowly, dreading this meeting more than the one with the city council.

Malcolm Kendall was standing by the front door when Waylon came around the corner. In retirement, he dressed more casually than when he'd been sheriff. But his western shirt could still stand on its own, and his boots were polished to perfection. He'd taken off his cowboy hat, and as Waylon walked closer, he noticed that there was more gray in his light brown hair. No doubt, he would have plenty more after what Waylon had done.

"Hi, Dad," he said.

His father nodded. "Son."

Waylon felt a tightening in his chest at the word. For a moment, he wondered if he was going to break down. Instead, he pulled out his keys and unlocked the door. He waited until they were inside his office before he spoke again.

"Did you want some coffee?"

"Not if it's anything like the coffee you used to make."

He forced a laugh. It came out choked and unconvincing. "It's still as bad." He started for his desk, but then hesitated. He felt awkward sitting in the chair when his father was there. His father seemed to read his hesitance and took the chair across from the desk.

Trying to postpone the conversation, Waylon took his time hanging his hat on the hook and sitting down behind the desk. He leaned back and folded his hands over his cramping stomach. "I guess you heard."

His father nodded. "Maybelline Marble called me."

Waylon was surprised. He thought it would've been Dan Wainwright who called his father. "I guess she was upset."

"Upset isn't the word. She was pretty ticked off."

Great. Ms. Marble was the one of the few people on the city council he'd counted on to be on his side. But it looked like even she was appalled at his disrespect for his office. "I'm sorry, Dad," he said. "I know I've disappointed you."

His father looked confused. "Disappointed me? I wouldn't say that I'm disappointed. I'm more worried than disappointed."

"I'm worried too. But hopefully the city council will be willing to listen to my side of things and choose to keep me in office. If they do, I promise I'll never cause another person in town to doubt my dedication to my job or keeping this community safe."

His father's eyebrows lifted. "You think I'm here because of the city council meeting?"

Waylon sat up. "You're not?"

"Hell, no. I can't tell you how many times I was called before the city council to deal with town gossip. It's all part of being a sheriff in a small town. People talk, and if you don't nip the gossip in the bud, it can get out of hand."

"It isn't gossip. I did let a fugitive get away when

he was right under my nose."

"From what I heard, you didn't know Holt Hadley was here."

"But I should've known. I should've known that something was fishy when I smelled the cigarette smoke and Spring was acting so weird. I should've known when Spring's trailer wasn't parked where it had been. But I let beautiful blue eyes and a pretty pair of lips keep me from reading all the signs."

His father sat back and studied him. "I didn't believe Maybelline when she told me how hard you've been on yourself since taking the sheriff's job. You were such a laid-back deputy, I figured you'd be a laid-back sheriff."

"You can't be laid-back when you're a sheriff. Not when you're responsible for the entire town. You taught me that. You were a hard-ass and people respected you for that."

A surprised look entered his father's eyes. "I hope that isn't why people respected me. I hope they respected me because I was levelheaded and fair. I realize I'm not a very personable kind of guy. Joking and teasing doesn't come naturally to me like it does to you and your mother. The people of this town knew that about me and didn't expect me to be something I wasn't. And they don't expect you to be either, Waylon. They voted you into office to replace me, not to become me. They loved you as the smiling, friendly deputy and were a little confused by the non-smiling, gruff sheriff you became."

"I was only trying to do my job of protecting this town."

"It is your job to protect the town, but don't

ever think you can accomplish that feat. Bad things are going to happen on your watch. That's just life. And things are going to distract you from doing your job. Your mama distracted me the very first time I pulled her over."

Waylon had heard the story of how his parents met a hundred times. And there was no comparison to his situation. "Mom was only speeding, Dad. Spring was harboring a criminal."

"From what Dan said, the feds didn't agree. After questioning her, they believed that she didn't know her father was running from the law."

"Then she fooled them. It's her bright smile. Spring can fool anyone with that bright, innocent smile."

Her father lifted an eyebrow. "That's what all this is about, isn't it? You're not mad at Spring for helping her father. You're mad at Spring for making a fool of you."

Waylon wanted to deny it, but he couldn't. "Hell, yeah, I'm mad at her. She had me believing that she was this honest, loving woman who cared about the people of this town. Who cared about me. But it was all a lie. Nothing but a lie!" He thumped the desk with his fist, and his half-naked cowboy screensaver came up. Another shaft of pain sliced through him, and he hated Spring all the more.

"So Ms. Marble was right," his father said. "You do love Spring."

His outburst had taken all his energy, and he slumped back in his chair. "I did. I don't love her now."

His father laughed. "You really are a greenhorn at love, son, if you think you can turn it off and on.

If you could, there would be a lot less heartache in the world. You love her. And you're hurt. I get it. Nobody likes to be made a fool of. But I'd rather be a fool in love than a fool who screwed up his one chance at happiness. Before you break all ties with this woman, you'd better make sure you're right. Because if you're wrong, you'll lose a lot more than a job." He got to his feet and pulled on his hat. "I guess I'll see you Easter weekend. Your mother is planning on making ham for dinner, even though she knows I hate it. But the grandkids love it, so my opinion is pretty much null and void."

Waylon got to his feet. "You aren't sticking around for the meeting?"

"No. I figure you can handle things quite well without me there. Besides, I'm done with town meetings." He winked. "I'd rather go fishing." His father came around the desk and gave him a big hug and a hard slap on the back before he walked out.

Long after Malcolm left, Waylon sat there digesting what his father had said. Not the part about him trying to fill his father's boots—Waylon had already started to figure that out—but the part about how he'd rather be a fool in love than a fool who screwed up his one chance at happiness.

Had he screwed things up? Had he been so angry about Spring making a fool of him in front of the entire town that he hadn't seen the truth? She claimed she hadn't known her father was running from the law. But how could she not know that something was going on when Holt had hidden in her trailer bathroom? That would've been a red flag for Waylon. Of course, he was a lawman who looked for red flags. Spring didn't look for anything but the good in people. And wouldn't she especially want to see the good in her father?

But if she hadn't lied about knowing that Holt was running from the law, then why did she leave without a word? Spring was tenacious. If she wanted something, she went after it. The assistant job was a perfect example. If she cared for him, why hadn't she stayed and fought for him? He sat there and mulled things over and over in his mind, trying to make sense of it. But it all came back to one thing: She left, so that must mean she didn't love him.

He glanced at the clock, then got up and grabbed his hat. It was time to pay the piper.

When he stepped into the town hall meeting room, he wished he'd gone fishing with his father. The entire room was filled with the residents of Bliss, and all eyes turned to him before the door even finished closing. Since he wasn't about to hide in the back, he took a deep breath and walked straight down the aisle that separated the groups of folding chairs and took a seat in the front row.

The town council sat at a table in front. The mayor usually sat in the middle chair with Joanna Daily and Ms. Marble on one side and Mrs. Crawley and Dirk Hadley on the other. Today, the mayor's chair was empty. Joanna Daily explained as soon as she called the meeting to order.

"There are two reasons for this emergency meeting today. One is to announce that Randall Gates has decided to step down from his position as mayor because it is taking too much time away from his ranch. We've elected a nominating committee and will be announcing the new candidates soon." She cleared her throat. "The other reason is due to a certain board member's insistence." She shot an annoyed glance at Mrs. Crawley. "And since she is the one who insisted. I feel like she is the one who should state her concerns."

Mrs. Crawley leaned up in her chair. "Thank you, Joanna. But I'm sure I'm not the only one in town who is concerned about the nefarious activities that have been going on right under our very noses. I'm appalled and think it's only right that our sheriff explain himself."

Waylon started to stand when Ms. Marble jumped in. "Sheriff Kendall doesn't have to explain himself. As far as I'm concerned, this entire meeting is nothing but a witch hunt." She pinned Mrs. Crawley with a direct gaze. "Cooked up by a witch."

Mrs. Crawley gasped. "Are you calling me a witch, Maybelline?"

"If the broomstick fits."

Mrs. Crawley's eyes narrowed on Ms. Marble. "I understand why you don't want a full investigation. From what I hear, you witnessed firsthand the depravity that's been taking place and did nothing about it. In fact, you condoned it."

Ms. Marble's eyes narrowed. "If we are going to investigate every act of depravity in town, then we're going to be having a meeting every day. And I'm sure members of your own family will be the first to be investigated."

Everyone in the room knew Ms. Marble was talking about Mrs. Crawley's daughter Winnie. And before things could get ugly, Dirk stepped in.

"Ladies, there's no need to fight. I'm sure Sheriff Kendall doesn't mind putting the gossip to rest by answering any questions you might have." Dirk glanced at Waylon. "Do you, Sheriff?"

"Not at all." Waylon stood. "As an elected official of this county, I am happy to address the issue." He turned to the crowd of people he'd grown up with. He'd spent most of his sleepless night trying to come up with what he was going to say to the town. But after talking with his father, he threw that speech out and spoke from the heart.

"I'll be the first one to tell you that I made a mistake. And the last few days, I've beaten myself up pretty badly for that mistake. You see, I don't— nor will I ever—take my job lightly. This town's wellbeing and safety is important to me. Not just as the sheriff, but as a member of the community. I was born here. I grew up here. And I hope to retire here. I love Bliss. I love the people of Bliss. But as much as I want to do a perfect job, I'm only human. I'm going to make mistakes. But I'll admit that letting a fugitive take refuge in my town is a pretty big mistake. All I can do is promise you that it won't happen again. If that's not enough for you, if that mistake has made you lose faith in my ability to protect you, then I'm willing to step down—"

"No you won't!"

Everything inside of Waylon froze at the familiar voice. Except for his heart. It seemed to beat in double time as he turned to the door.

CHAPTER TWENTY-THREE

SPRING SAW THE CONFLICTING EMO-TIONS in Waylon's eyes as she marched down the aisle. She saw the surprise, the confusion, and the pain. She also saw a glimmer of something else. That glimmer gave her hope. It gave her the strength to defend the man she loved.

She stopped right in front of him. "I won't let you step down. You love your job, and you're good at it. And anyone who doubts that needs to spend one day working for you. One day watching the hours you put in and the stress you put on yourself to make sure everyone in your town stays safe."

She turned and faced the people who were crowded into the room. "You should be ashamed of yourselves. You shouldn't be calling a meeting to condemn this wonderful sheriff. You should be calling a meeting to praise him for his dedication to his job." She pointed a finger at the crowd. "He cares about each and every one of you. He cares about your safety and your wellbeing and your happiness. And this is the thanks he gets? You call a meeting to kick him out of office?"

"Spring," Waylon said. "You need to let me handle this."

She turned to him. "No, Waylon—I mean, Sheriff Kendall—I will not stand by and watch the people of this town make a huge mistake. And getting rid of you would be a huge mistake. You are the most conscientious, hardworking, capable man I have ever met in my life. And it's my fault you're here and forced to be ridiculed in front of the town you only deserve respect from." Tears filled her eyes. "I'm so sorry for that. I'm so very, very sorry."

She turned back to the crowd as tears ran down her cheeks. "The reason Waylon didn't know my father was in town was because I lied to him. He trusted me and I betrayed that trust by not telling him that my daddy was here—by not telling him that Holt had stolen my Jeep and trailer. I tried to justify my actions by saying I didn't know my father was running from the law. But that was a lame excuse. I've known for a long time that my daddy is no good. I just refused to accept it. And now my gullibility has caused this great man"—she held a hand out to Waylon—"to be standing here today having to justify something that wasn't his fault. It was my fault." She tapped her chest. "If anyone should be judged and found lacking, it should be me. I'm the one who can't seem to do anything right. If I'd never come to town, everyone would be much better off."

Jonas stood up. "That's not true. I wouldn't have been better off. I was so depressed over Meg's death that I'd become a burden to Waylon instead of a good deputy. Spring made me realize that. She made me realize that Meg was gone, but I'm still here. And I have a son and grandchildren to live for."

"I'm better off too." Mrs. Miller stood up. "Spring was the first person who took time to really listen to me. She was the one who got me a job babysitting the triplets and got me out of my lonely house."

"And she helped in the diner when Carly was as sick as a dog," Stella Sanders said. "She's a terrible waitress, but she did her best."

"And let's not forget that she took care of our sheriff when he was sick," Joanna said.

Mrs. Crawley jumped to her feet. "Which is exactly why I called this meeting. It has nothing to do with Spring Hadley's father and everything to do with the inappropriate things going on in the sheriff's office between these two." She pointed to Waylon and Spring. "These two have been having an illicit affair for months."

Before Spring could think of how to address that, Waylon jumped in. "You mean this meeting isn't about Holt Hadley being in town?"

Mrs. Crawly waved her hand. "I couldn't care a less about some two-bit criminal passing through. What I care about is the morality of this town. And how our sheriff playing patty-cake with his assistant every night at his house reflects on our town." She raised her chin and stared down her nose. "And I saw the naughty things that were going on with my own two eyes. I was on my way to Joanna Daily's house to drop off the church Easter eggs and I saw Spring pull into the sheriff's garage. A few seconds later, the sheriff came out of the house and greeted her with a kiss that almost made me faint."

Spring cringed. This wasn't good. She could take the blame for what happened with her father, but she couldn't take the blame for Waylon kissing her. Unless she lied.

"It wasn't the sheriff's fault," she said. "You see I've had a major crush on the sheriff since I've come to town—"

Waylon cut her off. "Thank you, Miss Hadley, but I think I can take things from here." He gave her a soft smile before he turned to the townsfolk. "When I first took this job, I had big shoes to fill. I thought in order to fill them, I needed to become just like my father." He glanced at Ms. Marble. "But recently, it's been brought to my attention that I'm not my father. I'm not as strict. I'm not as somber. And I'm not married with three kids. If I feel like you've learned your lesson after a firm warning, I'm going to give you a second chance. If you've got a good joke to tell, I'd like to hear it. And if I meet a woman I enjoy being with, I'm going to flirt with her, date her, and even kiss her."

The thought of Waylon flirting with, dating, or kissing any other woman besides her didn't sit well with Spring. But she bit her lip and let him continue.

"Now if you have a problem with how I'm performing my job as sheriff, I will certainly address those issues and try to resolve them. But unless I'm breaking the law, you do not have the right to question my personal life." He looked directly at Mrs. Crawley. "Because what I do in my off-hours is none of your damn business."

Mrs. Crawley gasped and probably would've come back with something if Ms. Marble hadn't stood up. She sent Mrs. Crawley her sternest teacher look.

"I think that will be about enough out of you. The only reason I went along with the meeting was that I thought the gossip needed to be addressed and things needed to be cleared up. It looks as if the sheriff did a good job of clearing. Now that it's done, I, for one, would like to apologize to Sheriff Kendall for the gossip that was circulating. I'm sure that everyone in town will back me when I say that we're proud to have you as our sheriff. You're a good upstanding man and a strong leader who we all respect and love."

She started to applaud, and the rest of the town immediately got to their feet and joined in with a few shrill whistles thrown in. The only one not applauding was Mrs. Crawley. She looked like she'd eaten a bad apple. When the crowd had quieted, Joanna Daily tapped her gavel. "I move that this meeting be adjourned."

"I second that," Ms. Marble said.

People started filing into the aisle, but instead of heading for the door, they stopped by to talk with Waylon and slap him on the back or tell him a joke. Spring got lost in the crowd. Which was a good thing. Because now that the crisis was over, she felt pretty stupid for charging into the meeting like she was the cavalry. She should've known Waylon wouldn't need any help defending himself.

She weaved her way through the crowd to the door. Outside, it was a beautiful April day. The sun was shining and the sky was a vivid blue with plump white clouds trailing through it. The trees that lined the street were in full bloom and the flowerpots on the streetlamps were filled to bursting with spring flowers.

She took a deep breath of the fragrant air as she walked to Granny Bon's old Oldsmobile. Since her Jeep and trailer were still being held by the FBI, she'd been forced to drive her grandmother's car. Her sisters had wanted to come with her, but Granny had said it was something Spring needed to do herself.

As always, Granny was right. Spring would always have a special connection with her sisters, but sometimes a girl needed to be on her own to learn who she was and what she wanted. The sweet comments made by the people of Bliss had made her realize that, no matter what happened between her and Waylon, she was going to be okay. She was a strong, capable woman who loved people and loved helping them with their problems. And she intended to keep doing that, whether it was here in Bliss or in some other small town. She didn't want to live in a big city. She was a small-town girl through and through.

"Pardon me, ma'am." A cowboy came out of the diner and almost ran into her, spilling a little coffee from his to-go cup. The sight of the cup made her wonder if Waylon had gotten his morning coffee. The man could not sheriff properly without his caffeine. She had planned on heading to Dirk and Gracie's and having a conversation with Waylon after he got off work. But suddenly she realized that she couldn't wait that long to find out if Waylon could forgive her.

She turned and headed down the sidewalk toward his office. She unlocked the door with the key she still had. While she waited for the coffee to brew, she opened the blinds and made sure there was toilet paper in the bathroom. When the coffee was done, she filled Waylon's mug and carried it into his office.

His desk looked nothing like it had when she'd first started working there. In fact, it looked a little too messy. She set down the cup and straightened the papers that were scattered across it. She hesitated when she noticed the doodles on one of the pieces of paper. Tears welled up in her eyes and a thousand butterflies fluttered around in her stomach as she stared at her name surrounded by a chain of daisies.

The front door opened, and she quickly moved away from the desk.

"Yes, Tucker," Waylon's voice carried into the room. "You're in charge while I'm gone. No, you don't get to sit at my desk. I'll call you—" He cut off when he walked into his office and saw Spring standing there. He lowered his phone. "You're here."

She nodded at the mug sitting on his desk. "I made you coffee, but it sounds like you're leaving so I guess I'll have to put it in a to-go cup."

With his gaze pinned to her, he lifted the phone back to his ear. "I'll call you later, Tucker." He hung up and slipped his phone in his front pocket. "I thought you'd gone back to Waco."

"No, I—" A thought struck her. "You were coming after me?"

Instead of answering, he turned and closed the door. The click of the lock surprised her. Waylon never locked the door when he was in his office, only when he left. She didn't know if that was a good thing or a bad one. Maybe he just didn't want anyone walking in on the tirade he was about to dish out.

But he didn't look mad when he turned. His eyes looked soft and melty. "Yes. I was coming after you. A man would have to be stupid to let a woman go who is willing to defend him in front of an entire town. A woman who believes in him. And I'm sorry, Spring, that I didn't do the same for you. I should've believed you when you told me that you didn't know your father was running from the law."

"But you were right," she said. "Deep down I did know that my daddy was no good. I just didn't want to admit it . . . even to myself."

He took off his hat. His hair was endearingly mussed. "There's nothing wrong with looking for the good in people, Spring. Especially in your father. Everyone wants to believe that their dad is a good man. That's why I didn't tell you about Holt running a gambling operation. I didn't want to hurt you. But if we'd both been honest with each other, it would've saved a lot of misery."

"I've been pretty miserable," she said.

"Not as miserable as me. And speaking of honesty, there's something else I should've told you." He paused, and then blew out his breath. "Damn, I wish I was the type of poetic man who had a way with words."

Hope bloomed in Spring's chest, hope that what Waylon was about to say was what she'd been dreaming about him saying for weeks. She clutched her hands to her trembling stomach.

"I've never been that into poetry," she said. "Just plain ol' words are fine with me." Three plain ol' words to be exact.

Waylon nodded. "All I can tell you is that my life was dark and dreary until you walked into it like a ray of sunshine. At first, I was annoyed by your brightness because it illuminated everything that I was doing wrong. But once my eyes adjusted, I saw the brilliant beauty of your kind heart. And all I want to do is spend the rest of my life basking in its glow."

Spring held her breath and waited. Thank the good Lord, she didn't have long to wait.

"I love you, Spring."

The words flew like an arrow straight to her heart. And she flew straight across the room into his arms. "Oh, Waylon." She hugged him tight. "You're wrong. You are poetic. Those were the most beautiful poetic words I've ever heard in my life." She pulled back and smiled at him. "And I love you too. I think I've loved you ever since you stepped into my trailer."

He laughed. "You did not. You thought I was a stodgy sheriff with no sense of humor."

She scowled. "Okay, so maybe I didn't fall in love right away. For a couple weeks, you were just my grumpy boss that I had the major hots for. But then I realized that you aren't grumpy at all. You were just trying to be someone you're not to impress the town." She glanced back at the window and stepped away from him. "And speaking of the town, we better mind our p's and q's or Mrs. Crawley will call another town meeting."

"I think I've made it perfectly clear to Mrs.

Crawley and the entire town that what I do in my personal life is none of their business. And since I just called Tucker to take over, I'm off duty. And since you aren't my assistant—at least, you aren't until I rehire you—we won't be breaking any rules if I kiss you senseless."

She loved the thought of being kissed senseless by Waylon, but she also worried about him breaking the rules and getting in trouble. Before he could pull her into his arms, she stopped him. "But you can't rehire me if you want to date me. I know for a fact that there's a policy about dating your assistant."

He grinned. "But not about marrying her." Before her mouth could do more than form a surprised oh, he took her hand and knelt down on one knee. "I was planning on buying you a ring and taking you to a romantic dinner, but I can't wait a second more to make you mine. Please marry me and make my life Springtime all year long."

It was hard to get the words out with all the tears clogging her throat, but she managed. "Yes. A million times yes!"

He whooped as he stood and pulled her into his arms for a kiss. It was a tender but possessive kiss. The kind of kiss that says "I'm all yours and you're all mine." When he pulled back, she was crying like a baby.

She wiped at her eyes. "I guess you should know that I can cry at the drop of a hat."

He laughed and kissed her nose. "I happen to love how easily you cry. Like your smiles, your tears are signs of a caring heart. And I'm so glad you're entrusting that heart to me." He gave her another kiss that quickly turned heated. All she wanted to do was strip off his sexy uniform and have her way with him.

"Let's go back to your house," she murmured against his lips.

He took a slight nip of her bottom lip before he pulled back. "I have a better idea. He walked over to the window and closed the blinds with a snap that brought Spring out of her sensual daze.

"What are you doing?" she asked.

When he turned, his molten green eyes melted her like a popsicle on hot cement. "Something I've wanted to do for a long time." He unbuttoned his shirt as he walked toward her.

Her eyes widened. "Are you going to boink me on your desk?"

He slowly shook his head as he slipped off his shirt. "No. I'm going to make love to you on my desk. Do you have a problem with that, Miss Hadley?"

She sent him a sassy smile. "Not a one, Sheriff Kendall."

CHAPTER TWENTY-FOUR

SPRING WOKE WITH THE NAGGING feeling that something wasn't right. She lay there for a moment trying to figure out what it was, but nothing seemed out of place. Ever since Waylon had asked her to marry him, she'd woken up in his bed with him spooned close and his arm around her waist.

So what wasn't right?

She lifted her head to check on Sherlock and Watson. They were both sound asleep in Sherlock's dog bed. The kitten Mrs. Miller had given her was tucked securely between Sherlock's front legs. Spring glanced at the window. The sun shone brightly through the sheer curtains, which meant it was mid-morning. But she wasn't going to be late for work. Today was Saturday. The only thing she had to do today was—

She sat straight up. "My wedding!" She threw off the covers and jumped out of bed as Waylon came awake.

"W-what? What happened?"

"We overslept," Spring said as she raced to the

dresser and opened her panty drawer. "And it's all your fault. 'Just stay for a few more minutes,' you said. 'I promise I'll get you back to your brother's before midnight,' you said."

Waylon chuckled. "I had every intention of doing just that, honey. But then you wore me out with your lovemaking."

She glanced over her shoulder to see him sitting up in bed grinning like a cat that had gotten the entire carton of cream. "You're blaming this on me?" she asked.

He lifted his eyebrows. "You *were* pretty demanding last night. Any average man would be comatose this morning." He winked. "You're lucky your fiancé—soon to be husband—is above average."

"Urrrgh!" She threw her panties at him. "Quit being an arrogant jerk. Can't you see I'm having a meltdown? And quit looking at me. It's bad luck for the groom to see the bride before the wedding. Which is another reason I shouldn't have let you talk me into staying longer."

His eyes narrowed in thought. "Why is it bad luck to see the bride? That doesn't make sense to me. Wouldn't it be good luck to wake up and see the woman you're planning to spend the rest of your life with?"

It was hard to argue with that. Especially when he looked so sexy with his tousled hair, pretty green eyes, and naked chest. Her anger fizzled. She was going to spend the rest of her life married to this man. She glanced at the clock on the nightstand. That marriage started in less than five hours.

She quickly turned back to the dresser and grabbed another pair of panties. "My sisters are going to kill me. They were supposed to help me get ready."

"I'm sure they won't be too upset," Waylon said. "There's still plenty of time before we have to be to the chapel."

She pulled on her panties, then grabbed a bra. "Thus says the man who only has to shower and put on a tux. I have to get my hair done. My makeup. My nails—"

The bedroom door burst open. Summer strode in, carrying a to-go cup. "Rise and shine, lovebirds."

Spring stared at her. "What are you doing here?"

"What do you think I'm doing here? Autumn sent me to get our forgetful little sister."

"I didn't forget. I just overslept because—"

Summer cut her off. "I think I can figure out what happened. And I couldn't care less if you're late. I was the one who thought you should elope to Vegas, remember? It's Autumn who's in a major tizzy. She wants this day to be perfect."

Autumn *was* a perfectionist. She liked everything in its place and flawless. She was also a great planner. Which was why Spring had asked her to help plan the wedding. Spring hadn't wanted anything too big since they only had a little over a month to plan. But Autumn didn't do anything half-assed. Like a Martha Stewart whirlwind, she'd pulled together a wedding any bride would remember forever.

Feeling even worse for being late, Spring quickly slipped into a sundress as Summer handed Waylon a cup of coffee. "I figure you'll need it to survive the circus Spring and Autumn have planned for you. I'm assuming you're responsible for my sister

not being where she's supposed to be, Sheriff Way
. . . Too-Big-For-Your-Britches."

Waylon laughed. For some reason that Spring
couldn't figure out, he found her sister extremely
amusing. "She *was* right where she was supposed to
be." He took the cup and winked at Spring who
was slipping into her flip-flops. "With me."

Summer crossed her arms. "I've been going
easy on you because you're new to the family, and
because Granny Bon promised me a tongue lashing
if I wasn't nice. But I think you need to understand
that no matter how much you love her, I loved her
first." Before Spring could get too misty-eyed over
the sweet comment, she glanced at her sister. "Well,
don't just stand there looking stupid, Spring Leigh.
Let's get a move on."

As soon as they got back to Dirk and Gracie's
house, Autumn met them at the door. "Hurry! We
have a lot to do to make you the most beautiful
spring bride in Texas."

Spring didn't realize what a lot meant until she
had to endure it. Three long hours later, she was
finally showered, shaved, moisturized, manicured,
coiffed, and on her way to the little white chapel
where she would put on her dress and add the final
touches before she walked down the aisle.

Being late May, the bluebonnets were no longer in bloom. But other wildflowers blossomed in
bursts of yellows, oranges, reds, and purples that
matched the stained-glass windows of the little
church and the dresses of Spring's attendants. Her

bridesmaids were Gracie and Waylon's two sisters-in-law, who Spring met at Easter and just adored, and her maid-of-honors were Autumn and Summer.

All the women started out in the bridal room with Spring, but then Joanna Daily recruited the bridesmaids to help put the tulle and ribbon on the pews. Spring was glad for the time alone with her sisters. She was happy to be marrying Waylon, but also sad that she was leaving her sisters for good. Although Summer made it a little easier. Instead of being an attentive maid of honor, she couldn't stop talking about her new idea to save Seasons from bankruptcy.

"I really think this online personal shopper idea is going to work," she said as she sat in a chair and scrolled through her cellphone. "We can ship our client's clothes right from the store. And if we take our business online, you can work from Bliss, Spring."

"Spring can't help." Autumn dusted Spring's cheeks with blush. "She's going to be a newlywed and she has a full-time job as Waylon's assistant now that Gail's decided to stay in Lubbock with her mom." She glanced over her shoulder at Summer. "And would you quit lounging in that chair? You'll look like a wrinkled prune by the time you walk down the aisle." Seeing as how Summer's dress was purple, she *would* look a little like a prune if it got wrinkled. But Summer didn't seem to care.

"I can't believe that the county is okay with a married couple working together. Don't they worry about naughty sex going on in the office?"

"We don't have naughty sex in the office," Spring

said. At least they hadn't since the first time. After knocking the computer off the desk and breaking it, they had decided to keep their hormones in check while at work. She waited for Autumn to finish with the blush before she continued. "And since there haven't been any other applicants, the county didn't have much choice but to hire me. Besides, I'm the best girl for the job."

She was surprised when Summer agreed. "You are great with people. Which is exactly why I want you to help with Seasons' online customer service. Are you sure you can't answer a few emails at night?"

Spring wanted to help her sister, but Granny Bon had made her promise that she would stay out of her sister's new scheme. "Sorry, but I can't."

Summer sat up. "You don't think my new plan is going to work, do you?"

Spring didn't want to hurt her sister's feelings, but she couldn't lie either. "It's just that you don't know a lot about running an online business."

"Which is why I'm planning on getting help from Dirk's business partner."

Autumn dropped the hairbrush she'd just picked up and turned to Summer. "Ryker Evans? I thought you didn't like him."

Summer shrugged. "I don't like him. He's a smarty-pants computer nerd who doesn't answer texts promptly and doesn't have one scuff on his shoes."

Autumn picked up the hairbrush and started fluffing Spring's hair. "There's nothing wrong with keeping your shoes polished."

"Says the woman who cleans her running shoes.

Who cleans their running shoes? They're supposed to be sweaty and dirty. And I don't have to like Ryker to pick his brain."

"So he agreed to help you?" Spring asked.

"Not exactly. He's being a little difficult." She tapped out a text on her phone. "But I'll wear him down."

Poor Ryker. He didn't know what he was in for.

Autumn set down the brush on the vanity. "Your hair and makeup are perfect. Time to get your dress on." Spring's wedding gown was a princess-style with a beaded bodice and full tulle skirt. Once she had it on, Autumn smiled at her with watery eyes. "I wish Mama could see you."

Spring blinked back her tears. "I wish she could too."

Summer put down her phone and got up. "Don't you two dare start crying. We don't have time to fix makeup." But when she looked at Spring, her eyes held just as many tears. "Besides, Mama is here." She placed a hand on her chest. "She's here." She placed her hand on Autumn's chest. "And here." She did the same to Spring. Then she pulled both her sisters into her arms for a tight squeeze before she released them and slapped them on their butts. "Now let's go get Spring married."

The wedding was perfect . . . despite a few hitches. Spring forgot her bouquet and had to run back to the bridal room for it. She stepped on her dress on the way down the aisle and would've fallen if Dirk hadn't had a firm grip. She got distracted by how handsome Waylon looked in a tux and the pastor had to ask her a question twice before she answered with "I do." And when they were pronounced man and wife, instead of waiting for Waylon to lift her veil and kiss her, she flung her veil back and kissed him. He seemed to be fine with it. He held her tight and kissed her so long that people started whistling and applauding. Then he whisked her down the aisle and out the doors.

"Where are we going?" she asked. "We're supposed to stay here and take pictures in the chapel once everyone's gone. Then we need to head to Dirk and Gracie's for the reception."

"In this chatty town, it will take a while for the chapel to clear out, and there's something I wanted to show you." He led her down the path, then through the oak trees to where everyone had parked their cars. She knew what he wanted to show her as soon as they cleared the trees. It was hard not to notice the bright-pink vintage trailer hooked to the back of his truck.

"You got it back!" She gave him a happy hug.

"Dan Wainwright called a week ago and said you could come pick it up. And I thought I'd surprise you." He pulled back. "I also thought it might be fun to do a little camping in it for our honeymoon."

Her eyes widened. "You want to go camping in a pink trailer?"

"I can put up with a pink trailer as long as you come with it. I thought we'd do a little fishing, a little hiking, and a lot of Spring Flinging."

She looked into his soft green eyes and saw her future. A future filled with many adventures and plenty of love. "Sounds perfect to me . . . Alice."

Here's a sneak peek at the next book in *The Brides of Bliss Texas* series.

Summer Texas Bride will be out June 2018!

Summer Lynn Hadley had never been the type of woman to get all weak-kneed over babies . . . or men, for that matter. But she had to admit that her knees felt slightly wobbly as she took in the picture of Ryker Evans bouncing her three screaming nieces.

He wasn't wearing a cowboy hat like most of the men at the reception, probably because he didn't want to mess his perfect hair. And it was pretty perfect. Precisely cut on the sides and long and styled back on the top. Even with the bouncing, not one strand of rich chestnut brown was out of place. He'd grown a beard since the last time she'd seen him. Not a thick beard, but a close-trimmed one that framed his angular jaw and highlighted the curves of his lips. Those lips were tipped down at the corners as he glared at her.

"Don't just stand there," he said above the din of baby wails. "Do something."

She glanced at her nieces. She was good at a lot of things, but babies weren't one of them. "Like what?"

His deep sienna brown eyes widened as if she

were an idiot. "Make them stop."

"Umm . . . okay." She leaned down like she'd seen her sisters do. "Hey, Sweet Peas." The crying stopped immediately. Maybe she was better with kids than she thought she was. She smiled brightly. "Yes, it's your Auntie Summer."

The crying resumed. Louder than before.

Ryker glanced between her and the babies as if he was trying to figure out what had just happened. Fortunately, about then, her granny and sisters converged. Granny Bon took Lucinda. Autumn took Luana. And Spring took Luella. All the babies stopped crying immediately. But instead of Granny Bon getting after Ryker for making them cry in the first place, she turned on Summer.

"What in the world were you doing, Summer Lynn?"

"What was I doing? I wasn't doing anything. It was Ryker who scared the Bee-Jesus out of them."

Granny's eyebrows lowered. "Don't you dare take the Lord's name in vain, young lady. And that's my point. You weren't doing anything to help him settle the babies." Granny looked at Ryker. "I apologize for my granddaughter. Sometimes I think she has applesauce for brains."

Ryker smoothed down his tie that looked like it had been dunked in a horse trough. "I need to apologize for upsetting Dirk's daughters. I'm afraid I'm not very good with children."

"Three babies are hard for anyone to handle," Granny Bon said as she gave Lucinda a kiss on the cheek. "Even sweethearts like these. And I'm wondering how you ended up with all three of my great-grandbabies in the first place."

"That's my fault, Granny Bon," Dirk walked up with Gracie tucked under his arm. "I handed them off to Rye when I saw some yahoo of a cowboy trying to make a move on my woman."

"He was not making a move on me," Gracie said. "He was asking me about Summer." She smiled at Summer. "I think you have a cowboy admirer."

Summer glanced at the dance floor. "What cowboy?"

Autumn shook her head. "Don't expect her to notice anything or anyone when she has her phone. Who were you texting anyway? Everyone we know is here."

Before she had to answer, Sheriff Waylon Kendall walked up. As much as Summer resented him for taking her baby sister away from her, she had to admit that he loved Spring. His smile was sappy and his eyes dazed as he looked at his new bride holding Luella.

"I believe they're playing our song."

Spring looked back at him with the same sappy, dazed look. "And what song is that?"

"Every song for the rest of our lives."

Her sister giggled happily as she handed off Luella to Gracie and allowed Waylon to lead her to the dance floor. Summer rolled her eyes, then caught Ryker watching her. He'd been watching her all night. Not in a sexual way. More like a scientist that had discovered an unrecognizable specimen and was trying to figure out what to do with it. She couldn't blame him. She had gotten a little out of hand in the last month. But when she wanted something, she didn't let anything stand in her way. And she wanted something from Ryker.

"We should get the girls to bed, Dirk," Gracie said. She leaned up and gave Ryker a kiss on the cheek. "I wish we'd had room to put you up tonight. I hate the thought of you having to stay at the motor lodge."

"It's no problem," Ryker said. "Mrs. Crawley gave me the best room in the house."

Dirk hooted with laughter. "Lucky number 7 with the vibrating bed?"

Ryker smiled. His smile was shy and hesitant, like he was afraid to let it get to wide or bright. "That's the one. Although the vibrating mechanism doesn't seem to work. Neither does the coffeemaker."

"The bed's temperamental. It only works when it wants to. And don't worry about coffee. I'll stop by in the morning and take you to breakfast at the diner. You haven't lived until you tasted Ms. Marble's cinnamon swirl muffins."

"I appreciate the offer, but I probably should head back to Dallas bright and early." He glanced at his watch. "In fact, I think I'll call it a night."

Summer wasn't about to let him get away that easily. "You don't have to leave yet," she said. "It's not even ten-thirty. And you haven't danced one dance. In fact, why don't we remedy that right now?" She tried to hook her arm through his, but he jumped back like he was dodging a rattlesnake strike.

"Sorry, but I don't dance."

She scrambled for another way to keep him there. "Cake! Did you get a piece of cake? Ms. Marble is Bliss's resident baker." She pointed to Ms. Marble who was talking to Joanna Daily. "She's the little old woman in the wide-brimmed hat, and she made Spring's wedding cake. Four tiers of pure heaven, I tell you. You just can't leave without getting a piece."

"Thank you, but I'm not much of a sweet eater." He shook Dirk's hand. "It was a beautiful wedding. Tell your sister congratulations and thank her and Waylon for the invitation."

"Why don't you tell her yourself?" Summer said. "I mean it would be rude to leave without—"

"That's enough, Summer Lynn." Granny Bon cut her off, then hugged Ryker. "We're all glad you could come, Ryker. You have a safe trip home."

"Thank you, ma'am."

"I'll walk you out, Rye," Dirk said. They headed for the open door of the barn, and there was nothing Summer could do about it. Not unless she wanted a lecture from Granny Bon. Of course, she got that anyway.

"What has gotten into you? First, you leave that poor man to deal with three crying babies and then you call him rude right to his face."

"Well, he was rude. He should've told Waylon and Spring congratulations before he left."

"Dirk says that Ryker has always been a little socially awkward," Gracie said. "But he certainly made up for it with the wedding gift he gave Waylon and Spring."

"What did he give them?"

"Shares of Headhunters stock."

Summer was so mad she wanted to pitch a fit right there. Ryker gave her sister stock and he wouldn't even give her the time of day? That just wasn't right. And she wasn't about to let it slide.

"If you'll excuse me," she said. "I think I'll go

find my cowboy admirer and see if he wants to dance."

But she didn't head for the dance floor. Instead, she headed straight for the bar where she flirted a bottle of tequila from the bartender. She hid it in the folds of her dress and slipped out the open door of the barn.

The May night was a little chilly, but Summer had always been hot natured so the cool breeze was a relief. She spotted Dirk walking back to the barn. And not wanting to be interrogated by her little brother, she ducked around the side and waited for him to go back to the reception before she headed to the garage where she'd parked her red mustang.

She was just backing up when Autumn appeared in the red glow of the taillights. Summer slammed on the brakes, then rolled down the side window to yell at her sister. "Holy crap, Audie! I could've hit you."

Autumn walked up to the window. "Where are you going?"

"For a drive. The barn is way too hot and I need to cool off."

Spring would've called her an out-and-out liar. But Autumn was the more diplomatic of the sisters. The one who didn't have to say a word to make you feel guilty. All she had to do was look at you with those trusting blue eyes to get you to confess to anything.

"Fine," Summer said. "I'm going after Ryker."

Autumn released a sigh. "Can't you ever just give in, Summer? Do you always have to beat a dead horse?"

"I'm not beating a dead horse. I'm brow beating

a computer nerd. Two totally different things."

Autumn shook her head. "Even if you could talk Ryker into helping us, it's too late. We don't even have enough money to pay this month's bills. And with Spring married and living in Bliss, we've lost even more sales. You and I aren't exactly salespeople. Which is why we need to listen to Dirk. We need to sell the inventory we have left, pay our bills, close the store, and cut our losses."

It made sense. But Summer had never been sensible. Especially when it came to accepting defeat. "Quitting is what losers do. Success rarely happens the first time you try something. Success takes hard work and dedication. I'm a perfect example. Remember the first time I tried out for cheerleading? I scored the lowest of any girl trying out. But did that stop me from trying out the next year? Or the year after? Or the one after that? And finally, my senior year, I made the team."

"I think it was because Ms. Polk was tired of you harassing her about it."

"I didn't harass her. I just wanted to know what I did wrong and how I could improve. That's all I want to know from Ryker. I want him to point out any flaws in my new business plan and what I can do to improve it. But he refuses to even talk to me. I've had to resort to texting him numerous times a day to try and get his attention."

Autumn covered her eyes with her hand and groaned. "Good Lord. No wonder the poor man raced out of here like his tail was on fire."

"Well, I'm not letting him get away that easily."

Autumn lowered her hand. Her face held a resigned look. "Of course you're not. And I guess

I'll have to cover for you. Granny Bon would throw a fit if she knew what you were doing. And Dirk wouldn't be too happy either."

"Of course you have to cover for me. That's what sisters are for."

"What should I tell them?"

"Tell them that after seeing my little sister happily wed I got a wild hare to go to the little white chapel and make a wish for my own wonderful Prince Charming."

Autumn snorted. "As if they'd believe that. Everyone knows that you're not a princess waiting for her prince. You're the evil queen who is trying to figure out how to take over the world."

Some women might take offense to that. Summer wasn't one of them. She didn't mind being a little evil. And she certainly didn't mind being the queen in charge.

"Then just tell them that I went to the chapel to repent all my sins." Before Autumn could delay her any longer, she backed up and took off down the dirt road. She usually drove fast. Speed gave her a feeling of power and control. But tonight she drove the speed limit. She didn't want to beat Ryker back to town. Not that Bliss, Texas, would qualify as a town. It was no more than a grease spot on the highway.

Still, as she drove onto Main Street, Summer had to admit that it was a cute grease spot. Trees lined the sidewalk and planters of bright-colored flowers hung from each lamppost. There were the usual businesses named after the town. Bliss Grocery Mart, Bliss Feed Store, Bliss Pharmacy, Bliss Motor Lodge. Then there were businesses with original names like the Watering Hole Bar, Lucy's Place Diner, Home Sweet Home Décor, and Emmett's Gas Station. But the one business that made Bliss different from every other small town was The Tender Heart Museum.

Tender Heart was a series of fictional books written by Summer's great-grandmother in the 1960's. Lucy Arrington based the stories on the mail-order brides who had come to Bliss in the early eighteen hundreds to marry the cowboys who worked the famous Arrington Ranch.

Summer cared nothing about the history. And she especially didn't care about Lucy Arrington, the woman who had placed her only child, Granny Bon, in an orphanage because she didn't have enough guts to stand up to her family and raise Granny on her own.

She might not care about Lucy Arrington or the history of Bliss, but what she did care about were the books Lucy had written. Or not all the books as much as the final book in the series that had just recently been found. Once the book was published, the royalties would be divided between Lucy Arrington's living family members. Which included Summer and her family. The money would help her implement her plan to start an online business. But first she needed to get her ducks in a row.

She had made a mistake by jumping into the retail clothing business without putting much thought into it, and she wasn't about to make the same mistake. She had spent hours researching other online clothing companies, and she knew there was tons of money to be made. All she needed was a little help from someone who had been successful starting an online company. She'd tried getting her brother to help, but he'd refused. He had fronted them the money to open Seasons' clothing store, and he claimed the store had caused nothing but fights between his sisters. True, she and her sisters had fought about how to run the store. But they fought about everything. That was what sisters did.

The sign for Bliss Motor Lodge appeared, and she slowed and pulled into the parking lot. The rooms at the motel were set up in twos with a carport on either side. The carports now held vending and ice machines while the occupants' cars were parked in front of the rooms. A slick gray sports car was parked in front of room seven. The kind of car that went from zero to sixty in seconds. The exact type of car she planned on buying when she made her first million.

Not wanting to alert Ryker, she parked a few rooms down. She was halfway around the front of her mustang when she remembered the tequila. She went back and got the bottle. She hoped a little alcohol would loosen Ryker up. That's if she could get him to let her inside long enough to pour him a glass.

Her plan was to hold up the bottle of tequila and say something like "Since you left the party, I decided to bring the party to you." But when Ryker opened the door, her brain got short circuited by a pair of defined pectoral muscles and a ripped stomach that Granny Bon could've scrubbed clothes on.

"Holy crap," she said. "You've got muscles."

DEAR READER,
Thank you so much for reading *Spring Texas Bride*. I hope you enjoyed Waylon and Spring's story as much as I enjoyed writing it. If you did, please help other readers find this book by telling a friend or writing a review. Your support is greatly appreciated.

Love,

Katie

Overnight Billionaires:

A Billionaire Between the Sheets
A Billionaire After Dark
Waking up with a Billionaire

Hunk for the Holidays:

Hunk for the Holidays
Ring in the Holidays
Unwrapped

Anthologies:

Small Town Christmas (Jill Shalvis, Hope Ramsay, Katie Lane)
All I Want for Christmas is a Cowboy (Jennifer Ryan, Emma Cane, Katie Lane)

About the Author

Katie Lane is a USA Today Bestselling author of the *Deep in the Heart of Texas*, *Hunk for the Holidays*, *Overnight Billionaires*, *Tender Heart Texas*, and *The Brides of Bliss Texas* series. She lives in Albuquerque, New Mexico, with her cute cairn terrier Roo and her even cuter husband Jimmy.

For more on her writing life or just to chat, check out Katie here:

Facebook www.facebook.com/katielaneauthor

Instagram www.instagram.com/katielanebooks.

And for information on upcoming releases and great giveaways, be sure to sign up for her mailing list at www.katielanebooks.com!